# MARKED BY PAIN

The Marked Series

CECE ROSE AND G. BAILEY

# MARKED BY PAIN
## THE MARKED SERIES

## CECE ROSE & G. BAILEY

## Dedication

*For Gem, thanks for stalking me into friendship.*
*For Cece, thanks for making my stalking easier by being my best friend.*

# Prologue

## MACKENZIE

My fingers scrape across the ledge, holding on as the portal behind me pulls me to it. I glance down, only regretting doing so as I see the swirling blue portal and my grip on the edge of the stone slips. I hold in a scream as I try to get a better grip, only the blood on my hands is making it impossible to hold on. The stupid white dress I'm wearing only makes it harder for me to use my feet to climb up.

"Kenzie!" I hear Enzo shouting my name. I try to look up, only to have to use my hand to push a piece of rock that flies at my head away from me. I know Enzo won't stop looking for me, even in all the madness of the flying pieces of rocks that are being pulled into the portal, and the chance he could die before he finds me.

"Enzo, here!" I shout back, and I see him look over the edge of the cliff I fell down. Enzo jumps, landing right in front of me on the ledge and reaches down, pulling me up into his arms.

"I've got you, it's okay," he says and gently kisses my forehead.

"No, it's too late," I mumble, shaking my head and Enzo squeezes me tighter.

"You couldn't have changed anything about what happened," I hear Enzo say but I'm too distracted to tell him he is wrong as someone jumps down and lands next to us. Enzo turns us so he is slightly in front of me as we face my father. He stands there, with his long coat blowing in the wind and a happy expression. *He won.*

"It's your fault," I spit out and he laughs.

"Goodbye, Mackenzie. Thank you for everything you have done for this world, but I'm afraid we don't need you anymore," he says in a cruel, emotionless voice. I'm too late to stop him when he shoots a blast of air at me and Enzo, sending us flying off the edge of the ledge and down into the portal. The last thing I see is Enzo pulling me to his chest and his dark eyes as he looks down at me.

# Chapter 1

MACKENZIE

*S*itting with my knees to my chest, while staring down at the cold floor of the warehouse, I reject the man's offer again. I don't even respond, choosing to try and ignore his presence in the room. I don't want any part in this resistance or their plans. I've just got to be patient, and wait for the right moment to escape or for the guys to come for me. *I know they won't just leave me here.*

"We've been here for two weeks, Mackenzie. You need to give me an answer soon. The men are getting restless," he says. I've given him an answer, plenty of times, just not the right one. Well, the one he is after anyway. The door opens, and I look up to see Ryan enter the room. He whispers something to the man and then leaves, casting a regretful look in my direction as he leaves. *It's a bit late for regrets now, big brother.* The man—Alaric—stands closer. I think of him as Alaric, as I refuse to call him anything else. He is nothing else to me. As he towers over me, I advert my eyes back down, not wanting them to meet with the man whose eyes match my own. He sighs and turns back away from me.

"Mackenzie, my child, if you will not talk to me, perhaps you will listen to your lover?" he asks, as he continues walking to the door.

*Lover?* The confusion settles into my mind, and I look up, wondering what he could be talking about. Icy shock sets in, chilling me to my damn bones, as a familiar face looks down at mine. He's got a tight-lipped expression on his face, and his hair is messy. His glasses are noticeably absent, and I'm convinced he only ever wore them for show at school. He's never had trouble seeing during our training sessions, and I never saw evidence of contact lenses in his cabin. It was just a front, some-thing to hide who he really is. *What else was he hiding?* Running my eyes all over him, I'm feeling both happy to see him, but cautious about the way he has shown up. I bite my lip as I sink back against the wall, bringing my knees up in front of me again, more tightly this time. One question breaks through all the other thoughts that I feel rushing through my mind right now.

*What the hell is Mr Daniels doing here?*

"Kenzie," he says gently, making me remember the last time he used my nickname, moments before we kissed. I wonder if he uses it on purpose, to convince me to trust him.

"What are you doing here?" I ask him, and he sighs.

"Can we have a minute, Alaric?" Mr Daniels turns and asks him.

"Fine, but I want her to cooperate, I've had enough of this game she's playing," Alaric says firmly and walks out, slamming the door behind him. The harshness of the slam makes the whole wall slightly shudder. I look up as Mr Daniels kneels in front of me.

"Kenzie..." he starts, reaching for me, but I knock his hand away.

"Tell me what the fuck you're doing here, Mr Daniels? Why the hell would Alaric listen to you?" I question him, and he sighs, rubbing his hands over his tired looking face.

"Will you please listen to me? That means not trying to attack me before I can tell you the whole story?" he asks me gently.

"Depends what you're going to say to me, and it wouldn't be *trying*, Mr Daniels," I respond, and for some reason it makes him smile a little.

"I'm the leader of the rebels, well me, your father, and two others are," he explains. I stand up quickly, walking as far away from him as I can as the sting of betrayal begins to boil inside of me.

"You bastard! You did all this, didn't you? You let them take me away from the academy, it's your fault they kidnapped me! You knew my father was alive the whole fucking time!" I seethe and he shakes his head.

"I didn't know anything about the kidnap plan. I swear to you I didn't," he tells me, but I don't believe a word he says anymore.

"Was kissing me part of the plan? Making me fall for you?" I ask, my voice catching a little. He tries to move towards me, but I hold my hands out in front of myself in warning.

"Get out. Just get out, Mr Daniels," I spit out and he stops walking.

"You can hate me for lying to you, and I deserve that, but remember not everything's fucking black and white, Miss Crowe," he replies, walking out of the room. The door slams shut once again, as I fall to my knees and hold in the tears that threaten to fall. I don't know how long I spend staring at the floor, running every moment with Mr Daniels over and over in my mind, before coming to the conclusion that he played me. *He played me so damn well.* I stand up and walk over to the middle of the room. *Nobody else is going to save me now.*

"I know you can see me, and I want to see my father. Now," I shout and cross my arms, waiting for the door to open. I wait in silence. The seconds turn to minutes, and then the minutes turn into hours as I wait in silence. I pace back and forth in my little makeshift cell, waiting for him to come. Typical that as soon as I am ready to talk, he makes me wait. Eventually, I give up, going to sit on the air mattress on the floor, while I wait for someone to come in.

The door finally opens and I look up, watching Alaric as he strolls in, a satisfied look on his face. *About frickin time.*

"Well, Mackenzie?" he asks, as he leans back against the door, looking down at me. I stand up and walk across to him.

"What exactly is it you need me for?" I ask.

Instead of answering me, he gestures for me to exit through the door. I watch him, unsure for a moment, before daring to step through. When nobody stops me, I relax a little as he walks past me, and then leads me to another room. He opens the door and again gestures me inside. *Like he's herding freaking cattle.*

I motion for him to go first and he frowns, but steps inside first anyway. Following him in, I'm holding back a smile at my tiny victory. I refuse to let him be in complete control. I'll push where I can so I don't become a mindless robot while trapped here.

"Take a seat, Mackenzie," he says as I shut the door behind us. I grab a chair on one side of the table, and he sits at the other before beginning. "We need you, the twelfth power is crucial to our plan," he says.

"You've said as much, but what does it do? What do you need me to do?" I ask, crossing my arms across my chest defensively. I glance around at the small meeting room. There's a long table with chairs on either side, and not much else. Other than to shower, this is the first time I've been out of my cell since arriving here, so I appreciate the change in scenery. Even if it is just a trip to this bland-looking room.

"Mackenzie, do you think I am a fool?" he questions. When I don't reply, he sighs. "I cannot trust you with our plan just yet, but you need to realise why you should help us. The Marked Council are corrupt, mad with power. They make decisions for our kind that they should not. There are things you don't know, Mackenzie. They have forgotten our ways and allowed polluting of the bloodlines. They're making the rest of our kind weaker, so that they remain stronger. Encouraging people to procreate with humans, when they themselves do not. Why do you think that is?" he asks me, and I try not to snort. *Does he not realise how crazy he sounds?*

"Why?" I ask, trying to feign interest. I'm sure falling asleep won't help convince him I am on their side. I need to do that, if I want them to drop their guard enough that I can escape.

"Because they want to rule completely. Not as elected officials, but as a dictatorship over our kind. They want to weaken us all to the brink, so that only their selected few families remain strong," he answers.

"And what do you want?"

"We want to stop that. This is why we need you. You can stop this madness, and bring the power we need into our cause. We must overthrow the council."

"How am I meant to bring power into your cause? Why does it have to be me? How do you even know what my mark does?" I fire off my questions, not able to keep them in any longer.

"I cannot tell you everything yet, nor can I trust your change of interest now. But perhaps, soon I will be able to. I hope that over time you will see what we are doing here, that you will understand we are the good guys in all of this. We will be moving you to our main base tonight. If you try to escape during transport, we will lock you up tighter than Alcatraz. Do you understand?"

"I understand," I acknowledge.

"I'm not quite sure you do, but it does not matter. Either you will comply willingly, or we will make you."

"Is that a threat?" I ask, wanting him to just spit it out.

"Call it a motivator to behave accordingly," he answers, making me roll my eyes. "That's all I am going to tell you for now, Mackenzie. We'll be leaving in three hours," he says firmly, and it's clear this discussion is over.

"Where exactly is this base?" I ask anyway, but he doesn't answer. He stands and exits the room, slamming the door shut behind him.

# Chapter 2

MACKENZIE

"*W*hy are you working for them? Why are you a part of this stupidity?" I question, as we drive down the motorway. He stays silent, refusing to answer me like he has been doing for ages. I curse and stare out of the window. There are rebel-driven cars in front of and behind us, so we're completely surrounded. Not like I could escape Mr Daniels if I tried anyway. I need to wait for a better opportunity. Get back home to my parents, clearly the academy isn't safe. I need to tell mum about Alaric too. Now I know why she could never speak to him using spirit, it wasn't a lack of skill, the bastard was never dead.

"There are things you don't understand—"

"Save it," I mutter, cutting him off. Excuses

won't change anything. He betrayed my trust, pretended to care about me, all to help the rebels. The people who wreak havoc in our communities.

A car undertaking us, speeding up way above the speed limit, catches my eye. I watch the Mercedes with the tinted windows curiously as it slows down to keep level with us. *Is this another of their cars? What are they doing?*

The window rolls down and I try not to scream. *Easton.* The window rolls back up before I can even do anything about it. He speeds up again, before switching to the furthest lane. He's going to get off at the next exit, I'm sure. *Why?* I look around at the road signs and the answer hits me. There's a service station.

"I need to pee, can we stop?" I say, pointing at the upcoming exit.

"You cannot be serious," he replies, glancing across at me.

"Completely. What do you think I'm going to do, cause a scene in front of all the humans? Expose our entire race, just to help myself?" I question sarcastically. He seems to consider it a moment, before pulling out his phone. I can't help but glare at him. *He really shouldn't be using that while driving.*

"We're stopping at the service station. I need a

female member of the team to go into the restroom with her," he says, not bothering to greet whoever he's called. "No, I don't care if you think it's a bad idea, we're doing it," he barks, ending the call. He quickly switches lanes, and pulls off at the exit.

"Thanks," I mutter.

"Don't thank me," he says quietly.

"You're right, I shouldn't," I snap back. He turns to look at me, watching me for something as I stare right back, neither one of us wanting to say a word or break first. Mr Daniels stops the car, and places his hand on my shoulder. I don't move, but I glance at his warm feeling hand and then back up to his face. His soft brown hair, the cute dimples, and the alluring green eyes that I ended up falling for. I smile slightly, before placing my hand over his, linking our fingers and calling on my fire mark. He doesn't move as my hand gets hotter, hot enough to almost burn both of us.

"I deserve for you to hurt me, but I know you won't," he says quietly, and I glare at him.

"I could. You really don't know me that well, Mr Daniels," I say in an overly sweet tone, making my hand burn a little hotter, though still not enough to actually hurt him or leave a mark. I hate that he's right, that I can't make myself hurt him. *Not that I will ever admit it aloud.*

"No, you couldn't. Just like I could never hurt you, Miss Crowe," he says and I shove his hand away furiously, rushing out the car. I run my hand through my thick dark hair, pushing it from my face as I look around to distract myself from his words. I can't stop myself thinking how right he is, and how much I hate that, that he knows me so well, and that I clearly know so little of him. There are three cars parked behind us, blocking the entrance to the fuel station and as I look around, I don't see East's car. There are fields behind the fuel station, and nothing else, except for the small road that leads back to the motorway.

"Come on, twelve," I hear behind me, and I turn to see an older woman with long black hair and a serious expression. She has a water mark on her right cheek, not something that is uncommon in our kind, but its means she is powerful with that gift. I look over the car to see Mr Daniels get out, watching me with a neutral expression, none of the emotion showing that I saw in his eyes a second ago.

"Hurry up, Miss Crowe. And try to behave, I

don't want to have to come in there after you," Mr Daniels warns me.

"Fuck. You," I mutter slowly, keeping my eyes locked with his as he grins and folds his arms.

He doesn't reply as he turns and walks towards one of the other rebel's cars. I find my eyes tracing his tight ass in his jeans, and the muscular frame of his shoulders and back under his jumper. I pull my eyes away, knowing that I shouldn't be looking at him like that anymore, that he is the leader of the rebels. He is the bad guy, and yet, bad never looked so damn good.

I turn around, walking straight towards the entrance to the small fuel station. It's a blue building, with two places to fill up cars outside and the toilets are labelled with glowing neon lights above the door on a small side building. I hear steps behind me, and I turn my head to see the woman with the water mark following me, two men in black suits at her sides. *East better have a good plan.* I walk straight to the bathrooms, pushing the woman's door open, with the water marked woman following me inside.

Looking between the two stalls that have no gap at the bottom and tiny doors, and seeing one has the door wide open and the other is shut. There's one sink, and the room has a window at the end of the stalls. The window is small, but I think I could get out of it.

"Hurry up," the woman snaps, as she shuts the door to the toilets behind us, but I catch a glimpse of the two men standing guard outside before it closes. I go to the shut door, pulling it open and I see East sitting on the closed toilet seat, and his eyes widen in relief when he sees me. I put my finger to my lips, and he nods in understanding.

"Can you turn the tap on? I can't pee when someone is listening," I shout. The woman grumble something about spoilt princesses before I hear the sound of running water. I step forward at the same time East gets off the seat and reaches for me. We meet with our lips crashing together, his hands sliding into my hair and I hold in a little moan that threatens to escape when he pulls away.

"Kenz, I'm sorry, I'm an idiot. I knew something was up with Mr Daniels. That's why I reacted the way I did when I saw him with you," he whispers and my eyes widen in shock.

"What did you know? How?" I ask.

"I overheard a conversation, just the end bit and he said, *'It's all sorted, sister.'* I knew his sister is part of the rebels, and something must have been wrong for him to be talking with her," he tells me and I whack his chest.

"You should have told me, you let me live with him—" I start saying, and East puts a finger on my lips to stop me. I bite my lip, hoping I didn't speak too loudly.

"I only heard that two days before you were kidnapped. I was going to tell you, I just wanted the twins and Enzo's advice on how, because I knew how close to him you were," he tells me. "All of that doesn't matter now though, we need to get out of here," he tells me.

"How? There is a marked woman outside this door, and two men standing guard just outside the restroom," I ask and he grins. I watch in shock as he pulls a gun out of his jeans.

"We can't shoot her," I mutter, in a shocked whisper, a little horrified he would do something like that. It's so not East-like, at all. Human weapons are beneath our kind, only rebels normally use guns, as the council forbids it.

"It's a dart gun," he explains, seeing my concern. He kisses me once more quickly, as he slides around me.

"Where are the twins and Enzo?" I ask East

quietly, but he doesn't get a chance to reply as the door is banged on harshly twice.

"Hurry up, you can't be taking that long to have a pee," the woman shouts. East unlocks the door quickly, using his air mark to slam it open and we hear a grunt. We step out the stall to see the water marked woman on the ground. East shuts the door behind us and her eyes widen as he steps closer and lifts the gun, shooting her in the leg. She passes out quickly and we step over her.

"Use your air mark to lift yourself, Kenz," East tells me and I nod, watching as he floats up in the air and pushes the window open. He slides his body out, only his shoulders struggling to get through, and I call my air mark the moment he disappears. I float upwards, grabbing hold of the window and letting go of my mark in my mind as I pull myself through. As I start to slide forward, half my body hanging out the window, I realise I didn't think this through. I fail at stopping myself as I fall face first through the other side of the window and large hands catch me.

"You go backwards through a window, Kenz," East laughs quietly, putting me down. I look up into his hazel eyes that are full of humour and something else I can't really think about right now.

"I'm not good at escaping, I need a lesson in that," I whisper back as I step away.

"Maybe my brother could give you lesson. Not in escaping, but listening to what you're told," I hear a familiar voice say behind me and I turn to see Mr Daniels walking over with the brown-haired rebel that tried to kidnap me. I look between them, seeing the resemblance, and realising instantly that she must be Mr Daniels' sister. *Why didn't I figure it out before?*

She smirks at me, before lifting her hand and sending a wave of air into both of us. East goes flying with me, catching me around the waist, and making sure I land on top of him as we crash to the ground.

"Shift and run," East whispers and I do as he says without thinking about it, calling my mark and rolling off him. My change is quick, painless, as my body shifts and I land on four paws. East jumps into the air, shifting into a massive hawk with long grey feathers and a sharp looking beak. My wolf doesn't let me look long, my mind blurring as she suddenly growls loud, turning and looking at Mr Daniels and his sister as they run over to us.

"Verity, don't hurt them," Mr Daniels says, though she doesn't respond as she keeps her eyes locked with mine. She shifts suddenly, morphing into the large snake I've seen before. I run at her, growling as I ignore the shouts from Mr Daniels as she lifts her large head and dives at me. I jump to the side, thinking I've avoided her, until I feel a sharp pain in my hind leg. I turn to see the snake biting me, green venom dripping from her teeth and my wolf collapses to the ground with a loud howl.

"You will kill her! Stop, Verity!" Mr Daniels shouts, his voice desperate, and a blast of air sends the snake flying away from me, her teeth ripping my skin as she goes, and making my wolf whine out in pain. The pain blurs everything, the night sky, the sound of a hawk screeching above me. It becomes more and more fuzzy, until I can't focus on any of it anymore.

I'm not sure what is real and what isn't as I look around. I try to imagine my human body, try to return back to normal so I can fight, but nothing happens. As everything starts to go dark, I look up into the sky to see a hawk flying down towards me, its hazel eyes glowing with anger.

## Chapter 3

MACKENZIE

"If she dies, I will kill you. I don't give a fuck if you're my sister. I don't give a fuck about any of it," I hear Mr Daniels snarl out, his voice dripping with enough anger to make me shiver. I'm surprised he is talking to his sister like that. The anger in his voice can't be faked, and I remember someone pushing the snake away from me before she could kill me. *Did he save me?*

"I told you already, I didn't have control over my snake. She wouldn't let me—" Verity whines back, and Mr Daniels interrupts. I'm glad he did, her voice sounds so fake and sweet, like she is pretending to be a child. A whiny one at that.

"I don't believe the shit you told Alaric. Get out." I hear the sound of a door opening and shutting, before the room goes silent. I don't move, feeling groggy as I try to blink my eyes open.

"I know you hate me, *I* hate me for the things I've done. But if you ever felt anything, let me explain—" Mr Daniels begins, but the sound of the door opening again stops whatever he was going to tell me.

"What the fuck did Verity do to my sister?" Ryan's voice demands, and the sound of the door slamming behind him makes me push my eyes open. I quickly shut them again, thankful I wasn't facing the direction of the door. I want to know what Ryan has to say when he doesn't think I'm listening.

"You heard the report, same as everyone else," Mr Daniels growls in response.

"I want to know what really fucking happened, I know the report was all utter shit. Is Kennie okay?" Ryan asks as I hear him walking closer.

"She'll be fine. She tried to escape, so Verity stopped her. That's all there is to tell," Mr Daniels says coldly.

"Get the fuck out," Ryan barks, and I hear him step closer. He must be right up against Mr Daniels. I hear him stand.

"What did you just say?" Mr Daniels whispers in a low, deadly tone.

"I said, get the fuck out. Stop sitting there as if you give a shit about my sister, and get the hell out of here. I don't want her to be stuck seeing your face when she wakes up," Ryan replies.

I hear sounds of scuffling, and quickly sit up, opening my eyes. They both freeze, looking in my direction.

"Just go," I say, staring at Mr Daniels.

"Miss Crowe—"

"I said go, I don't want to hear whatever shit you've got to say!" I snap, cutting off his excuses before they can form.

"Fine," he replies curtly, but his green eyes are blazing. He turns and leaves, banging the door shut behind him. I look around at my new prison. *At least this one is nicer to look at.* An actual bed with crisp white sheets, pale blue wallpaper, and a dresser with a TV on top. If it wasn't for the steel-looking door, it would almost be a little homey. If minimalism is your idea of home décor anyway.

"Kennie," Ryan begins, drawing my attention back to him.

"Ry, I don't want you here either. Just go away," I say quietly.

"I didn't mean for you to get hurt, but we need you," he replies, his voice sounds sincere. For some reason, the sincerity pisses me off even more. *How could he be so stupid?*

"Well I have been hurt, and you've caused that to happen, so live with it. Just freaking get out of here, and leave me alone."

He turns to leave, but pauses. "I came to tell you about East," he replies quietly without turning back. *Shit.*

I sigh, not wanting to continue this conversation, but needing the information about East. "What about him?" I ask.

"He's here. They captured him, well, rather he let himself be captured when he saw you pass out," Ryan answers.

"He just let himself be captured? I need to see him!"

"That's not going to be possible, Kennie. You know they won't let you near him," he says carefully, turning back around to face me. I turn away, I can't look at my brother's face without feeling furious. "Look at me."

"I don't want to, I can't." I cross my arms over my chest stubbornly. I feel like we're kids again, but this isn't an argument over who ate the last cookie.

"I'll see what I can do. I can't make any promises, but I'll try and find a way for you to see him," he says, and I turn to face him.

"You need to get us out of here, Ryan," I reply bluntly. He doesn't say anything, just looks at me blankly. "East is your best friend, and I'm your damn little sister. Doesn't that mean anything to you? You can't be okay with us being kept prisoner here. Who even are you anymore? Help us escape, please, Ry," I plead, hoping to get through to him.

"I can't do that, Kennie. You're still my sister and I'll keep you safe here, but we need you for this rebellion to happen," he answers with a sad smile.

"Then get out, I can't look at you anymore," I snap, feeling the rage already building up again.

"Fine. I'll check in later to see how you are." Ryan steps back, slowly at first, as if not wanting to leave.

"I'd rather you didn't," I say, glaring daggers at him.

"I know, but I'll come and see you all the same. Get some rest," he says, pulling the door open to leave. "See you later, Kennie."

"Bye, Ryan."

# Chapter 4

MACKENZIE

*P*ulling on my navy-coloured jacket, I freeze as the door opens. Slowly I turn on the spot to face the man who has just entered.

"Good morning, Mackenzie, I trust you slept well," Alaric greets, as he steps into the room.

"Yes, being held captive always helps me sleep soundly," I reply sarcastically, as I zip up my jacket. The chill of the room requires a jacket whenever I'm not huddled under the covers.

"Well, perhaps once you see more of what we are trying to accomplish here, you'll no longer be a captive. How about a tour?" he asks, flashing a salesman-like grin at me. It's all I can do not to smack the smile off his face. *Liar.* Mum would be horrified to find out he's here, alive, corrupting her son, and now trying to do the same with me. I miss her and my other dads so badly. I miss Kelly. I miss East, Locke, and Logan. I even miss Enzo, the asshole. "Well?" he drawls.

"I suppose I can't say no," I mutter.

"It would be better if you just tried to understand, Mackenzie. Just come take a walk with me, meet some of our people. Understand why they are choosing to be here," he offers.

"Fine." *What's the worst that could happen?* "But I want to see East. I'll play nice and be good, listen to whatever you have to say. I'll go on a frickin' tour of this place, but after, I get to see East," I add, figuring it's worth a try.

"Easton Black?" he questions.

"Who else?" I ask, rolling my eyes.

"You can have ten minutes with him," he offers.

"Twenty," I counter, pushing my luck. I need all the time I can get with East, to retain my sanity in this place.

He looks at me calculatingly. "Fifteen, final offer," he offers, smirking at me.

"Fine, fifteen minutes with East for a damn tour where I listen."

"Let's get to showing you around then." He

heads back through the door, and seeing no other option, I square my shoulders and follow him.

―――――――

TRAILING AFTER ALARIC, I'm surprised at how boring a rebel base can be. I expected weapons, equipment, people doing military style drills. Instead I find classrooms, dorms, a dining hall, and even children running around. At first, I'd been shocked, but now I'm just bored. I was confused at the fact I'm allowed to freely walk around the base, not chained up in a dungeon or anything, but then I saw the wall surrounding the whole place. A patrol walks along the top on a loop, and it's heavily guarded at all times. It's the only sign of what this place truly is, that I've seen. A hand waves in my face, and I turn to look at him.

"Are you listening, Mackenzie?" Alaric asks in a pained tone.

"Sure I am," I answer automatically.

"What did I just explain?"

"Umm..." I trail off, not having a clue what he's said.

"Alaric, Simon needs to speak with you." I turn at the sound of Mr Daniels' voice, and I stare at

28

him. Despite how mad I am, and how much his betrayal hurts me, I can't help but notice how good he looks in his workout clothing. It makes me think of our last training session, and what happened between us there.

"Is it urgent?" Alaric gives a pointed look at me. *Subtle.*

"Would I be coming to get you right *now*, if it wasn't?"

"Fine. You can finish showing her around, while I go speak with Simon," he instructs. He turns to me. "Goodbye, Mackenzie."

"Bye," I reply blankly, happy that he's leaving, considering I feel so uncomfortable around him. I watch him leave, until he's turned the corner and is out of sight.

"So, where's the good stuff?" I ask Mr Daniels.

"Good stuff?"

"Yeah, the weapons of mass destruction, people being tortured, that kind of thing," I say.

"Nowhere, there's nothing like that here, Miss Crowe. What kind of organisation do you think we are?" he asks dryly.

"The kind that breaks into a school and attacks students," I snap back.

"What?"

"Your psychotic sister, she tortured a student. Don't act like you don't know!" I turn away from him, and start to walk off. I don't get far though.

"What do you mean she tortured a student?" he asks, grabbing my shoulder and pulling me back around to face him. I see the serious look on his face and sigh.

"I mean, she used the pain mark on one of the students in my year," I answer. When I look into his green eyes, all I see is her, so I look down.

"She wouldn't do that. If that had happened, it would have been in the report filed by the school with the council. I didn't read that in the report," he says firmly.

"I saw her do it with my own eyes; are you calling me a liar?" I ask, clenching my fists, only just keeping control over my powers.

"No, of course I'm not. I just don't understand why she would have done that. The instructions were clear, if a student got in the way, they were to knock them out, and leave them out of the way of harm. Are you sure it was her?"

"Does anyone else wander around in double leather and turn into a snake?" I ask incredulously.

"I need to talk to her about this." He shifts uncomfortably on his feet. I don't like it. He normally acts so confident, so sure of himself. It's unnerving to see him unsettled.

"Whatever. Face it, you're part of a group that condones torturing kids, and wants to cause chaos among our kind. These people are human haters! These are the kind of people who want to kill off the humans, or enslave them!" I shout.

"No, it's not like that at all, Miss Crowe. They just support segregation between the species, to keep the blood lines purer. They believe in keeping our society separate from theirs, but no longer in hiding."

"Don't you mean *you believe?* You're a leader of this stupid group." I lean back against the wall, as I watch his face for his reaction.

He looks around before answering, as if he doesn't want anyone to hear this. "I'm here for different reasons than most. I don't necessarily disagree with what they stand for, but I have more motivating reasons for being here."

"And those are?" I ask, prompting him to continue. *I need more of an answer than that.*

"You're pushing your luck, Miss Crowe."

"When do I not? I think you owe me an explanation; considering everything I deserve that at least," I say, staring him down.

"I'm here for Verity, and because of the council."

"What do you mean, because of the council?" I ask, narrowing my eyes.

"The council came for her when they found out she was a part of this, and our parents fought them while she escaped. They were killed, and branded traitors, just for protecting their own. All they wanted to do was save their daughter. But the council thinks they can do whatever they want," he seethes.

"I didn't know about that," I say softly, placing a hand on his arm. I'm not able to stop myself, seeing the pain on his face. He shrugs me off.

"I don't need your pity."

"It wasn't pity," I mutter, and then suddenly I'm pinned to the wall. His body is pressed up against mine, as his hands hold mine above my head. I freeze, barely remembering to breathe.

"What was it then?" he asks quietly.

"I was comforting you. Gods only know why after what you've done, but I hate seeing you in pain," I whisper.

"I didn't want to hurt you," he whispers back.

"Then why did you?" I ask, not able to cover the cracking in my voice.

32

"There are things you don't understand…things I can't explain yet."

"That's just shit, and you know it," I snap, closing my eyes to escape the intensity of his stare.

"I do. And I'm sorry, Miss Cro--Kenzie. I'm sorry, Kenzie," he breathes. I feel his lips press over mine, and I know I shouldn't, but I kiss him back. I'm desperate for him to be closer as he releases my hands to rest his on my hips. I tangle my hands in his hair as I kiss him back furiously, letting out all of my emotions into it. The anger, the pain, everything. Sense slams into me, my eyes fly open and I call on my air mark, shoving him back and into the opposite wall.

"I'm sorry too. That shouldn't have happened," I say, turning on my heel and walking back to my prison cell of a room. He calls after me, but I ignore him. Increasing my pace, I practically run away.

I can't trust him, and I can't trust myself around him right now.

## Chapter 5

MACKENZIE

"Down there," Alaric says, pointing to the plain, grey door at the end of the corridor. It has two guards standing outside, guns clipped to their belts and serious expressions marring their faces. I don't bother saying thank you to him or even looking his way, instead choosing to just walk forward, and wait for the guards to unlock the two locks on the door.

I've waited all morning for my father to come and get me, so I could see East. I tried not to replay the kiss with Mr Daniels over in my mind, or the story he told me about his parents. I understand why he's angry with the council, but I have no idea whose side he's truly on. His actions and words tell me two different stories.

"I will wait for you, we need to talk, Mackenzie," Alaric says from behind me in a cold tone. I turn and give him a single nod wondering why he looks so happy. As much as I hate the man, my father, I'm thankful he's letting me see East. The guard opens the door and I walk in, looking at the small bed, toilet, and sink in the otherwise empty, white-painted room. East is lying on the bed, a thin, scratchy-looking blanket covering him. He sits up slowly as the door is shut behind me. All the air leaves my body when East's hazel eyes lock with mine.

"What the hell did they do?" I exclaim, looking at the range of blue and black bruises all over East's face. His lip is cut, his hair is messy, and yet he still smiles at me like he doesn't have a care in the world. The blanket falls to his lap as I stare in shock at the state he's in. *Why did they do this? Why didn't they heal him?*

"Come here." He opens his arms, and then flinches in pain, moving his hand to hold his ribs as he coughs. I run over, sliding onto the bed and putting my hand on his face. There's dried blood on the side of his head, and I reach up to see the deep cut.

"I'm okay," he says, coughing, even as he lies to me.

"That's a load of shit, East. I'm not blind," I mutter, wiping a tear away that I didn't notice had fallen. I'm guessing East doesn't have the healing mark, so he can't fix himself, but I know I can try. Even if I'm not as good as Kelly at this. *Where's Kelly when I need her?*

"I can heal you," I say, already calling my healing mark. I feel my power flow through my hand in a crashing wave of energy, as I feel how badly he's hurt. My hand burns hotter and hotter, as I feel all the pain he is in, the way it hurts him to breathe, and it makes tears fall down from my eyes harder. *I can't believe that anyone would hurt him this bad.* It takes a while to heal all the marks on his face and the deep cut on his head, before I can gently push him back on the bed and slide his shirt up. I have to hold in a flinch when I see the shape his chest is in from the damage. I can actually see two of his ribs, pushing against his skin, and there are actually shaped bruises where someone must have kicked and punched him. They didn't just use marked powers, this was more than that. *They wanted him in pain and alive, but why?*

"You aren't strong enough to heal all of me, I'm

just glad to see you're okay Kenz," East murmurs, and I shake my head disbelievingly. "I was so worried," he adds.

"I'm going to heal you, and then I'm going to have a chat with my father. I have a feeling he won't like our chat, because the bastard must have had something to do with this. Now stay still," I tell East, who laughs.

"When did you get so bossy? I remember when you couldn't speak to me without bright red cheeks and looking at the ground," he chuckles as I press my hands on his ribs and calling my healing mark again. We sit silently, sweat dripping off my forehead as I struggle to heal the four broken ribs, and flinching every time one of them clicks back into place.

"I was shy around you, because every time you spoke I couldn't focus. You're sexy East, with the panty-melting voice," I tell him honestly, while avoiding looking at his face, making him laugh as my cheeks flush.

"I always thought you were beautiful, even when I knew I shouldn't have been looking. But you were so shy, I never realised how smart, kind and brilliant you are," he says, and I look up.

"Really?" I ask in a whisper, not believing he

really saw me as anything other than the annoying sister of his best friend.

"Really," he smirks and I look down with a smile, concentrating on healing the last one of his ribs.

"Stop," East says, pulling my hands away suddenly, and reaching up to wipe a finger under my nose. His hand moves away, and I see the blood that must be dripping from my nose smudged across his finger. East passes me a tissue as he looks at me with concern.

"Who did this?" I ask, placing my hand on his cheek.

"I don't know who they were, three of them came into my cell this morning wearing masks. They were all marked, but they didn't use their powers," he spits out, "I didn't stand a chance against them all, and my powers wouldn't work. I tried to call every one of my seven marks and they wouldn't respond," he says.

"I'm going to kill them for it," I promise and he leans forward, lightly brushing his lips against my own.

"Have you seen Ryan?" East asks as he leans back on the bed.

"Yes, have you?"

"No. I knew he had a slight problem with us being together, but I thought I knew him. He was my best friend and he hid this from me," East says.

"He's my brother, and I didn't have a clue," I say commiseratively.

"We can't have that much time left and I wanted to tell you something—" East goes to say, but the door is banged three times before we hear the sound of a key unlocking.

"Don't do anything I can't protect you from. Please don't be reckless here, they need you alive, but they will lock you up if you do anything. But trust Mr Daniels. Promise me you will trust him," East pleads with me and I lean back, processing his words over and over in my mind. *Did he just ask me to trust Mr Daniels? The man he hates, the one who did this to us?*

"What? Are you crazy? He's one of the leaders here!" I whisper harshly, just as the doors are opened. I turn to see a guard pushing the door open and waiting.

"Trust him," East tells me once more, and I look back at him with confusion. East leans forward, sliding his hand roughly into my hair and pulling me to him. He kisses me harshly, demanding, and utterly irresistible as his lips devour my own.

"What was that for?" I ask breathlessly, as he pulls away and keeps our forehead pressed together.

"I'm done wasting a single second with you, Kenz," he says, kissing my forehead as I lean into him.

"Come, Mackenzie," I hear Alaric say from the door and I stand up, turning away from East to look at my father. He looks just like me, the same tanned skin and the same dark hair. I even notice that we have the same shaped eyes, but none of the similarities we share mean that we are anything alike. All I feel is a burning anger as I walk out the room, following him. My father walks away, towards the other door we came in, like he hasn't got a care in the world. Like he didn't let some of his people beat up East. I call my air power, pulling my hand back and slamming a wave of air at my father's back. He flies across the room, slamming into the wall by the door with a loud grunt.

"Stop!" I hear a guard shout behind me and I turn, calling my protection mark, making a wall between us and the guards before they can get to me. One of them runs straight into it, bouncing off the ward and onto the floor. *Let's hope they don't have the protection mark.*

"What are you doing?" my father roars as he stands up and I turn, putting my hand out in front of me, and calling my fire mark.

"My mum used to tell me stories about you," I start off, moving one step closer, "Do you even think about your wife? The mother of your children?" I ask but I don't need him to actually answer. I know he doesn't, he couldn't really care if he let her believe he was dead, even for a day. You don't let someone you love think you're dead, not when it destroyed my mum like it did.

"Every day, but my responsibility to the world and the resistance has to come first. Put the fire down, and tell me what has you so upset," my father tries to reason with me, speaking to me like I'm a damn child. It's almost funny enough to make me laugh. The time for acting like a parent is well past, and I have three dads who did that. Not this pretender. I chuckle, putting my other hand in the air and calling another fire ball.

"Is that what you tell yourself so you can sleep at night?" I shake my head. "Mum once told me how weak you are to fire, because you never got the water mark. You can't put the fire out," I smirk, making the balls in my hands grow.

"Mackenzie…" he says, edging his way backwards towards the door.

"Did you honestly think I would let you get away with hurting East?" I shout, and he shakes his head. I throw one of the balls of fire at him, and he jumps to the side, and it burns the wall instead.

"I have no idea what you are talking about," he shouts, getting up.

"Don't lie to me!" I screech, calling another fire ball and ignoring the wave of dizziness that I feel when I do. The door opens behind my father, and Mr Daniels walks in.

"What's going on?" he asks, looking between us. My father simply smiles, an evil smile that tells me he thinks he's just won. I don't believe a word he says about not knowing that they hurt East, his face says it all. I wonder if he did this to test Mr Daniels, to see if he will side with him or me. It's no coincidence that he happened to just come in here right now. This whole thing had to be a plan by my father.

"I'm sorting out a big problem, it's best you get

the hell out of my way, Mr Daniels," I say and throw the fireball in my left hand at my father. A wall of water appears in front of him as he runs away towards the door, the water stopping the fire ball with a hiss. Steam blocks my view of them both. And then, the water shoots out towards me. I gasp for breath as the water rushes over me, shoving me back up against the wall. I feel like I'm drowning, but as quickly as it came, it goes away. The water pulls back, and I glare at Mr Daniels as he steps through the water. It drips down his hair and shirt, and I hate that he's so much more attractive wet. *Why can't he look like a wet dog or something? I probably look like a drowned rat.*

"Why did you attack him? I thought you could behave for one day. I should have known better," he asks, wiping his face of the water. I look away from Mr Daniels, through the water wall, and I see my father running away out the door. That's all my father is good at apparently, running. I look back at Mr Daniels, who silently watches me, assessing me for something as I ring the excess water from my hair. I realise that the water couldn't drown me, not with my water mark, but I'm still pissed he would use his powers against me.

"You chose to side with him and not me. You don't trust me, and I don't trust you anymore either. Stay the hell away from me," I say, feeling like my heart crushes even more with every word. I never should have trusted him, I shouldn't have fallen for him. I don't care what East might say, that I might be making the wrong decision, but I know he doesn't trust me. He chose to side with my father over me, and I can't forget that.

"I do trust you, Miss Crowe, but you do not understand the bigger picture here. Just know that I'm on your side. You know how I feel about you, I won't give up what we have together; it is worth fucking fighting for!" he says, making my heart pound against my chest.

"Then you have a big fight on your hands, Mr Daniels, and it's not one you're going to win," I reply coldly, walking around him and straight to the wall of water.

"We will see, Miss Crowe," the bastard shouts, just before I go through the water and I wish I didn't hear him. He doesn't stop me, the cold water is a welcome relief as it hits me, mixing with the tears that fall from my eyes so that no one will see them.

No one stops me as I walk down the corridors,

keeping my eyes low and dripping water onto the shiny floors with every step until I get to my room. I step in, slamming the door behind me and fall to my knees, tears streaming down my face.

*I never should have trusted him. What's worse, is that I have no idea who I can trust anymore.*

# Chapter 6

MACKENZIE

"Training? You want me to train?" I scoff at Alaric.

"Yes, Mackenzie; I think it would be best for you to train with our recruits. I know you'll come around eventually, and I do not see the point in segregating you now with that in mind," he replies. I look at him like he's mad. I think he really might be, but how does he convince everyone else that he's normal?

"I'm not doing it," I say flatly, as I sit back down on my bed. I don't take my eyes off him though, I don't trust him not to attack.

"Just come and watch the training then, you don't have to take part," he suggests, his tone light. His face, however, is calculating as it watches me.

*What is he planning?* "What else are you going to do? Sit here and mope all day?" *That was my plan, actually. Mope, mope, and mope some more.*

"I'm not sure, what do kidnap victims normally do for fun?" I ask.

"You're my child, it's not really kidnapping, is it? More like you've been grounded, don't you think?" he muses.

"Fuck you. You're not my father; I have three dads, and you are nothing compared to any of them," I snap. I haven't spoken to them since being taken, it's so hard losing all contact with the parents I'm so close with. I don't need to listen to him pretending to be a parent. He's nothing more than a donor to me.

"You cannot deny what's in your blood, Mackenzie Crowe," he says smoothly, not seeming at all affected by my words. "Now stop being childish, and come at least to watch the training. I will have men drag you in there if I must, but I'd rather not. We don't need to make a scene." He steps back out the door, as if he just expects me to follow.

I want to stay put, to kick and scream the whole way if they try and make me go. But I know it'll do no good, only tire me out. An opportunity to escape

47

could come at any time, I can't waste my energy. Sighing, I stand back up and follow him out of the room.

He's already halfway down the corridor, not slowing for me to catch up. Cursing under my breath, I jog a little to reach him, so I don't get lost in the mess of this place. He leads me from the building, and cuts across the grass outside to another building I haven't been in yet. Inside the building is a large gym-like hall, on one side it has been set up like a classroom, with desks and a whiteboard facing them. There are currently five people sitting in the seats, but they're facing away from me so I can't see their faces. The other side looks like it's for more physical training, with blue mats littered across the floor. There are rocks, and various other things lying across the ground too. *For earth practice, maybe?*

Alaric clears his throat, and one by one, the faces turn my way. The first two faces are unfamiliar to me, but the next three make my heart crash wildly against my chest, and my hands shake at my sides.

*What the fuck. Why are Enzo and the twins here?*

I look between all their faces trying to understand what they are doing here. Enzo's face is a blank mask, nothing I can read there. Logan looks sheepish, and Locke looks downright guilty. I have no idea what they are planning, why they're here, or who's side they are truly on. The only thing I am becoming certain of, is that I cannot trust anyone. They could betray me like Mr Daniels did. I won't let myself be fooled. Until it's clear whose side they are on, I have to keep them at arm's length.

"Why don't you take a seat, Mackenzie? I am sure the person leading the class will be here momentarily." Alaric gestures to the seating. Gritting my teeth to stop myself from snapping, I walk over and take one of the empty seats. I sit at the back, away from the others. "Fantastic, I have to be off now, but I will speak to you later. I'd love to hear what you make of your first day in training, sweetheart," he says, and then turns and leaves.

"Sure you fucking would," I mutter under my breath as I watch the door close behind him. I'm glad he's gone, but the room I've been left with isn't much better. *What the hell are they doing here?*

The seat to the left of me pulls out, scraping across the floor. I look up, seeing Enzo sitting down. His dark eyes are watching me intently, as he looks me over. It's not an emotional look, more like a clinical assessment.

"Hey, Crowe. How are you doing?" he asks quietly, as he pulls off his leather jacket, letting it fall against the back of his chair. I try not to notice how his black t-shirt clings to him, but it's a losing battle. He looks good, even though I'm pissed I can admit that.

"Just frickin peachy. It's not just Mr Daniels here I have to worry about, you're all here as well!" I snap back under my breath, but all the heads in the room have turned to watch us regardless. The two faces I don't recognise are watching curiously, whereas Logan and Locke look tense.

"You need to understand, we're all on the same side here—"

"Really? You're going to give me that same bullshit he did, too? Just leave me alone," I cut him off angrily.

"Kenz," Logan says, standing, and moving to sit on the seat directly in front of mine. He twists it to face me though.

"Don't 'Kenz' me. How long have you been a part of this?" I demand.

"We just joined, the three of us. Daniels has been looking to recruit us all for a while now, apparently. But when his cover was blown at the school, he came to get us. Gave us all the option to join and come with him, East said no…" he trails off with a guilty look to match his twin's.

"You know what happened to him, don't you? The state he was in when I went to check on him, it was awful. You can't seriously be okay with this?" I question him.

"It's not what I think that matters, Kenzie. East made his choice, and we made ours," Logan says. I look across at Locke, who has looked away, and is staring at the door.

"What about you, Locke? Anything to say?" I ask, ditching the quiet tone. I don't give a fuck who hears what anymore.

"There's nothing to say, Kenzie. The rebels are trying to make things better for our kind, we want to help in that," he answers, but it sounds forced. I frown. *There's something not right here. They can't all surely be brainwashed like this? What did Mr Daniels do to convince them all?*

The sound of the door opening makes me turn my head. I stand up, knocking my chair back onto the floor as I gape at the figure making their way into the room.

*No. This cannot be happening. Not her, she can't be one of them, too.*

She walks across the room until we are standing face to face, she gives me a small smile. I can't help but feel stabbed in the back, and in the heart, both at once. I stare at my closest friend, the girl I grew up with, and I feel sick.

"Hey, bestie. Are you settling in okay?" Kelly asks. She reaches out and pulls me into a hug. I stand there numbly, just letting her hug me. I'm too shocked to resist. I look over her shoulder, spotting Ryan sauntering into the room.

*What's next, my mum and other dads show up too?* I shiver at the thought.

"Are you cold?" she asks quietly. Coming to my senses, I pull away and look at her accusingly.

"How could you do this?"

"Ryan's been asking me to join for a while now. Now that everyone's here, I have no reason to say no," she answers meekly.

"Your freaking parents are on the council!" I snap. "Have you lost your mind…have you all lost your minds? What the freaking hell is wrong with you all? The rebels are criminals, they want to kill or enslave the humans. You know I went to a human school as a kid, Kelly. You even hung out with some of my human friends with me. Do you really think they're worth less than us? Who even are you anymore?" I question her, watching as she steps back from me, looking shocked at my outburst.

"Don't talk to Kelly like that," Ryan growls, walking over and wrapping an arm around her shoulders comfortingly.

"What about you then, Ry? You went to a human school too, had human friends? How can you look at yourself in the mirror?" I ask, glaring at him.

"Just because you got along with the humans doesn't mean I did, Kennie. I never fit in with them, they knew there was something different about me, about our family. I once let slip about having more than one dad, and the humans, you wouldn't believe how they reacted. As if anyone else's relationship is their business, but to them, it was sick and wrong. They were awful; they don't understand us or our way of life. They wouldn't accept us for what we are if they knew, so why should we accept them?" he questions.

"You don't know how the humans would react. Sure, maybe some of them would react badly. But there are good humans too, just like there are good and bad marked," I say, trying to make him understand.

"Crowe, maybe save the family drama for another time. Ryan is supposed to be leading the training," Enzo says in a bored tone.

"You cannot be serious." I look at Enzo disbelievingly.

"Yes, I am, actually," he says. He then gestures to the other two recruits in here. "They didn't come here to listen to your drama or negativity, take your damn seat and let Ry get on with the training."

"I can't believe you, I can't believe any of you…" I say, trailing off as I back away.

"Just sit down so we can get on with this," Ryan says, in a calmer tone than before.

"Screw you, screw all of you!" I shout, turning away as I run to the door, I pull it open and rush out, running as fast away from the training room as I can.

I'm not sure where I am heading until I get there. I stand outside the building nervously, before entering. As I make my way inside the building, I'm surprised how nobody stops me. The guards standing outside of the steel door are watching me intently when I get to them.

"Give me five minutes, please?" I plead, they don't answer, just ignore me. I feel like screaming.

"Let her in to see him," Mr Daniels' voice comes from behind me, making me jump.

"Are you sure, sir?" one of them asks, as he looks behind me nervously.

"Yes, I'm fucking sure. Don't question me, Jacob," he snaps. Jacob moves to the side, opening the door for me to enter. I rush in, not bothering to say thanks. After what he's done, he doesn't deserve it. Seeing East's face, as he looks up at me, makes me feel like I'm home, and everything's okay. He stands and pulls me tightly into his arms, and I cave, letting the tears fall from my eyes.

"It's okay, Kenzie, it'll be fine. We'll find a way out of here," he says soothingly, as he rubs my back.

Easton Black, the guy I'd fallen for when I was a kid, is the same person as he always was. Good, gorgeous, and he knows right from wrong. No matter who else has turned, East hasn't. East is my refuge in this place, the only one I have left. I lift my head up, pressing my lips to his, and he holds me tighter as he returns the kiss.

*East is still himself, and he's still on my side.* I repeat it in my head, like a comforting mantra over and over. The words make me feel safe. I pull away and take a seat on his sorry excuse for a bed, and he slides his hand in mine when he sits down next to me. He doesn't say anything else, just holds on tightly. A silent show of support and comfort, knowing words couldn't possibly make things better.

And in this moment, I think I love him for it.

# Chapter 7

MACKENZIE

"I didn't expect to find you ready and awake this morning, Mackenzie," my father says as he opens my door. I meet his eyes in the mirror I'm staring in.

"I have training," I reply with a neutral voice. I look back at myself in the mirror, pulling my long black hair into a high ponytail. I smooth down the black leggings and tank top I found to wear. I have knee high black boots on that I found and fell in love with, and after applying a little makeup, I think I look decent. I need to look halfway good to have the confidence to get away with all the pretending I have to do today. *I'm not letting them beat me anymore, I'm damn fucking stronger than this, and East needs me to be strong enough to get us both out of here.*

"It's good to see you are coming around to our ways, maybe we could have dinner tonight?" he asks and I turn around, smiling, and hoping it doesn't look as fake as it feels.

"That would be lovely," I reply, and he turns around, walking out my room with the guards following. I walk out, shutting my door behind me, before following him down the endless corridors to the training rooms outside.

"Good luck today, my daughter," he says, smiling like he's won the lottery. I walk into the training room and the door shuts behind me with a loud bang. I hold my head high when I see Ryan, Enzo, and the twins talking in the middle of the room. They all turn to look at me slowly, hearing the door shut, but I don't look away. Remembering the same thing I told myself last night as I couldn't sleep. *I'm stronger than anything they can throw at me.*

"Kennie, you came back," Ryan comments and smiles widely as I walk over. I don't reply as I go to the middle of the first row of seats and sit down on a chair. I cross my arms, leaning back in my seat, and raising my eyebrows at them all as they stare at me.

"This is training, right? Or is it just making pointless statements class? Or staring at me class?" I reply. Enzo chuckles darkly, before coming over and sitting in the seat directly behind me. Locke and Logan give each other a worried look, before going to sit behind me next to Enzo.

"Today's training is going to be——" Ryan goes to say, before the doors open once more, cutting him off. I turn to see Verity walking in, her high-heeled boots clicking across the floor, and she's dressed in all leather again. Her brown hair is up in a bun, her face is covered in makeup, and I hate to admit that she looks good.

"I've decided to join the training class today, Ry," she tells my brother, using a friendly nickname that makes me grit my teeth. She then moves to sit in the row of seats behind me. I turn to see her sat right next to Enzo, her eyes trailing up and down him before turning to look at me, with a small smirk. I catch Enzo's dark eyes as I turn around, noticing how they watch me and the fact that he didn't look once at her. It only makes me feel a little better, before it makes me remember how I'm not meant to like him. *He betrayed me.*

"Fine, Verity," Ryan says, moving in front of the white board again, "Today's class is going to be about learning how to use your powers in combat. We will pair off, and take five minute rounds before switching," he says and I jump when Enzo kicks the back of my chair. I turn in my seat to glare at him, but pause when I see Verity's hand on his arm.

"Kennie, you're with me. Come on," Ryan tells me as I stare at her hand, anger burning through me, and all I can think about is pulling her stupid high heeled boots off, and stabbing her with them.

"Kennie?" Ryan asks as Enzo moves Verity's hand off his arm and I look up at him. He shakes his head, before kicking my chair once more.

"Are you deaf?" he asks me.

"No, I just can't hear people that speak constant bullshit. All the people in this room seem to have a talent for it," I say and then mutter more quietly, "That and being brainwashed idiots." I get up before Enzo can reply to me. The twins watch me, both of them look like they are bursting to say something, but can't. *It's weird*. I walk over to where Ryan is waiting by the whiteboard. I look back to see Logan and Locke walking off together, and Enzo with Verity. I try not to let it bother me, even if it takes everything in me to look away from them all.

"Let's go outside for training, it's a nice day, and you might want some air," Ryan suggests.

"Oh, so we're allowed outside? Here I was

thinking I was a prisoner, but apparently I got it all wrong," I say in an overly sarcastic voice, as I walk next to Ryan towards a door on the other side of the room.

"Kennie, I know what your twelfth power is. I know that you need this rebellion to survive. You're acting like such an ungrateful brat for everything my father, your best friend, and everyone else that cares about you has given up, just to keep you alive," he snaps at me, before walking faster towards the door. I stop in my tracks, anger burning through me as I call my air mark, slamming a gust of air into the mats leaning against the wall and sending them flying into his side. He falls to the floor, the mats falling on top of him, and he pushes them away with his own air power.

"You're such a brat. Are you ever going to grow up?" Ryan huffs as he stands up.

"I'm the brat? Me?" I laugh as Ryan stomps over to me and grabs my arms, shaking me lightly.

"Stop it. Just stop and listen rather than letting your ego ruin a good thing for you," he snaps.

"I will never side with your rebellion, never. Not after what they did to East, and if this really was the right way, why would East be locked up and beaten?" I whisper, not wanting anyone else to hear.

"Kennie—"

"Stop calling me that stupid nickname, stop trying to control me," I seethe, losing control of my power and a wall of flames appears from my hands, without me calling my mark. The flames slam into Ryan, setting him on fire as he flies across the room. I quickly call my water mark, and make a wave to wash over him as I stand in shock.

"Ryan!" I shout, as I snap out of it, stopping my water mark as I run over to where he is on the floor, burns covering his clothes and arms.

"What did you do?" Locke shouts as he runs over to us, placing his hands on Ryan, and they glow white.

"Get Kelly," I shout at Enzo as he runs over. He nods, quickly turning around and running for the door as it's opened. Kelly walks in, holding a clipboard that she drops when she sees us and runs over, sliding onto her knees.

"Ry? Baby?" she whispers as she pushes Logan out of the way, putting her hands on Ryan's chest, and she starts glowing as tears run down her face. We all stay still as she heals him, none of us making a single sound.

"What happened?" she asks me, once she moves her hands away and to my surprise, there isn't a

62

single burn on Ryan's skin. He's still passed out, but he's alive, thank the gods.

"I lost control, I didn't even know I was calling my fire mark until it was too late," I say, and then I look down at the floor, not able to meet Kelly's eyes. "I didn't mean to hurt him."

"Maybe you should learn more control then, Twelve," I hear Enzo say as I stand up, walk over to him, and whack my hands against his chest as he looks down at me.

"Maybe you shouldn't be such a jerk," I say, moving to hit his chest once more and he grabs my hand, pulling me against his chest. All the air leaves my body as he leans down, putting his head so close to mine, I'm practically moulded into him.

"I wish we were in the woods again," he whispers, reminding me of the time we kissed. Reminding me how he responded to me, how nothing about that night felt fake. I pull away from him, seeing his eyes, so dark, as I stare into them and feel lost.

"It was an accident, I know you would never do that to your brother. We should get him back to his room," Kelly says interrupting us, and making me quickly step away from Enzo as I look over at her. She has her hand on Ryan's face, tears still streaming down her cheeks, and it makes me pause for a second. Despite how she betrayed me, and everything that happened, she loves him. That I believe completely in this moment. Logan walks over, holding his hand up, and making Ryan float in the air as Kelly stands up.

"Kelly, if you walk by his feet and Kenzie you go by his head, I can float him back to his room. Just rest your hands near in case he falls," Logan states. I step away from Enzo, walking over to my brother's head and Kelly steps near his feet. I keep my hands out as Logan uses his power to move Ryan out the room, and I look back once to see Verity standing close to Enzo, touching his arm again. I swallow the sickness I feel rising to look ahead as we go down the corridors. People move out of our way, not stopping us as we walk in time with each other.

"Kelly, get the door," Logan says, and she turns, opening the door quickly. I step back while Logan places Ryan on the bed and turn to shut the door behind me, as Kelly sits on the bed next to him, holding his hand tightly.

"Can I speak to you in the bathroom?" Logan asks quietly, but doesn't wait for me to answer as he grabs my hand and pulls me to the other door in the room. He opens it up, pulling me inside and shutting the door behind us, before turning the lock. Logan walks over to the shower, turning it on, and coming back to me as I lean against the door.

"Will you get in the shower, Kenzie?" he asks, and I laugh.

"Are you joking? Not a chance," I reply as I cross my arms. He growls as he picks me up. I fight him, not using my powers because I don't want to hurt him, but he throws me into the shower before I can get free. The warm water pounds down on me as Logan steps into the shower and closes the glass door, shutting us in together. I let my eyes travel down his white shirt, and notice that it's see through now, and shows off his muscular chest, the way he has that v line that dips into his jeans. My heart pounds as I finally look up, seeing his eyes watching mine as his wet hair drips all over his face.

"What the hell are you doing, Logan?" I ask breathlessly, only seconds before he presses me against the shower wall and kisses me. Forgetting stupid things like asking questions, or the fact I'm mad at him, I kiss back, sinking my hands into his wet hair. The warm water from the shower continues to drench us even more, soaking our clothes right through as we continue to kiss, and forget the world.

He pulls away, making a pained sound as he does, as if he resents the fact he has to move away. "Fuck, I've wanted to do that since we got here, Kenzie," he breathes, and some sense snaps back into me.

"What the fuck do you think you're doing! You can't just act like nothing has happened, act like you haven't betrayed me and East. You don't get to do that!" I seethe, pushing him further away, so he's standing on the opposite side of the shower now.

"Listen I brought you in here to explain--"

"Explain? You think you can just talk your way out of this? No way, Logan. Get out of my way, I'm leaving. Where the fuck are the towels?" I question, as I try to push past him. He grabs my wrists and pulls me back, pinning me up against the wall of the shower again. After what just happened with Ryan, I concentrate on keeping my powers under control, taking deep breaths.

"Let me go," I demand, once I have calmed myself enough to think straight.

"You can go, but you have to hear what I have to say first. Please, Kenzie," he pleads. I look into his eyes and sigh, seeing the sincere look in them.

Whatever he has to say, he truly thinks it's important.

"Fine," I say reluctantly. Sighing agian as I lean back against the wall, the water still pouring down over us.

"I'm not meant to be telling you this, fuck I may be ruining the whole escape plan here, but I can't stand seeing you hurt like this. I can see why East did what he did now, I think his job may have been the easier one in hindsight." Logan swallows, and I can see how nervous he is to continue.

I link my hand in his. "Explain."

"We're here to get you out. Me, Locke, Enzo, and Kelly. Mr Daniels is on our side now too, but he can't break his cover, it's too important."

"What do you mean he's on our side *now?*" I ask.

Logan licks his lips. "Well, he really was a part of the rebels, but that's changed now—"

"Like fuck it's changed!" I snap. "Have you not seen him, running around like he's the boss here?"

"Keep your voice down, Kenz. We should be okay to talk in here, but don't risk it any more than we have to," Logan whispers harshly. "Look, he found out something that changed it all for him, something he wouldn't ever allow to happen. It's to do with you, we can't let the rebels have you, we just can't."

"I don't understand, is this about the twelfth mark?" I ask.

"Yes, no, kind of? It's what could happen by using it," he says.

"What do you mean, what could happen? What does my mark even do?"

"I don't know, he won't tell me what your mark does. What he did tell me, is that using it could kill you, Kenzie. There's no records of anyone using the twelfth mark and surviving. We have to get you out of here," he answers.

"Shit. They're planning on killing me? Does Ryan know this?" I ask frantically.

"He's been told that you will live, that they have a plan to ensure you survive using the mark," Logan says.

"But that's a lie?"

"It's untested, there's no guarantee their plan would work, and I'm not convinced they care if it fails to keep you alive. So long as they get use of your power first, that's all they care about."

"But Ryan thinks I'll be okay? He's not...he's not okay with me dying, right?" I ask in a small voice, the betrayed feeling rushing through me already.

"Hey, it's okay," Logan says as he pulls me close. He holds me tightly to him. "Ryan thinks you will live, he wouldn't do this otherwise. You're his little sister and he loves you."

"Then why don't you just tell him that I might not live?" I ask and Logan swallows thickly. "You think he won't believe you? That he might reveal your plan to them?" I question, making a guess.

"Yes, he's been completely pulled into this, Kenzie. He's basically brain-washed. Your dad sent Verity to Ryan a couple years ago, and she's been slowly poisoning him for years."

"Shit. How did we not realise?" I ask, looking up at Logan.

"We couldn't have known. Don't blame yourself, gorgeous, this isn't your fault," he says, and I sigh. I don't believe that, but now isn't the the time to argue that point.

"What's the plan? And if you're here to break me out, why is East locked up right now?"

"I can't explain the plan now. Just be ready to go at any moment, Kenz," he says, and I nod. "East is…East is locked up because he couldn't deal with the thought of you feeling like we had all abandoned you, that we all betrayed you. He didn't want you to feel alone in this. He knew his rescue attempt

69

was likely to fail, but he accepted that, because he knew then you'd feel like at least one of us was still on your side. He said it would help keep you strong and motivated to escape, so Daniels gave the plan the okay. He wasn't happy about it though, he knew it was likely that East would get hurt," Logan explains.

"He knew they would hurt him, if he got caught trying to rescue me, and he did it anyway? To stop me from being alone? He did that for me?" I question softly.

"He did. Fuck, I wish I'd done it. Seeing you hurt, thinking we all betrayed you, it was so hard, Kenzie, I couldn't do it," he whispers, leaning down his face closer to mine.

"Really—" my words are cut off as his lips claim mine again, and his body moulds into mine as I'm pressed against the wall. He releases my hands to move his own into my hair, gripping it as he holds me firmly in place.

The shower door is slammed open, and Logan slides me down his body as we turn to face Locke who is holding the door. He reaches in, switching the shower off.

"As much as I don't want to interrupt this, or how much I want to join in, Ryan is awake and asking for you," Locke says gently, and I step around Logan, leaning up and pressing my lips to his.

"Thank you," I say, leaning back as he stares at me in understanding. He realises I know everything in one look. Maybe because I'm not glaring at him like I have been since they got here.

"So where are the towels?" I ask looking down at my dripping wet clothes, and making them both smile. I ring my hair out, letting the water drip onto the floor.

"I dunno, I like the wet look on you," Logan says as he steps out the shower, and my eyes trace his body, wishing we hadn't been interrupted.

"Same here," I grin, just as Locke hands me and Logan some towels he found. We dry off the best we can before walking out the bathroom, and I see Ryan sitting up on the bed. He looks pale and tired, but there are no burns, which I'm thankful for. I stare at him for a while, not knowing how to process that he's being lied to. That nothing he knows is real, and all I feel is sorry for him.

"Kennie," Ryan says, sitting straighter.

"Careful, Ry," Kelly warns as she watches me from the other side of the room with her arms crossed, wearing a worried expression.

"I'm sorry I've been such a brat, I know I have been and that's changing now. I'm going to try and get along with our father, to help the rebellion," I say, lying as there's no way I'm helping them. No, I have to escape before they try to kill me. But at least I know I can trust three of the four people in the room now. Just not my brother.

"I get it, and I'm glad that you're finally seeing what's right in front of you. You can trust me, you can trust us," he says and waves a hand. "Come here," he asks me. I walk over, sitting on the bed next to him and holding his hand. I just hope he doesn't hate me and everyone else when he realises just how wrong he is about this place, and about our father.

# Chapter 8

MACKENZIE

"*I* didn't think you would come, not after the incident with Ryan earlier today," my father says when he opens his door that I've just knocked on. I smooth down the tight red dress I'm wearing, plastering on a fake smile as I look up at him.

"It was an accident, and I've learnt that I need more control over my emotions and powers," I say as he steps out the way and waves me into his room. The entrance hall is large, as big as my bedroom with two doors on either side. It has gold carpets, gold walls and expensive looking paintings on them. The whole entrance hall looks like it costs more than my old home.

"Well you are young, and that is what we are

here for, to teach you control," he tells me and I smile tightly. I will show him control when I shove my fist into his face.

"Hello, Miss Crowe," Mr Daniels says as he steps out the door to the left, dressed in a suit that makes him look more attractive than should be allowed. His brown hair is styled out of his green eyes, which seem to lock onto my own. I want to forgive him for everything he has done, but I still can't get the thought that he runs this place out of my head . That he betrayed me from the second we met, even if he decided to side with me in the end. What changed his mind? Was it knowing I would die?

"Mr Daniels," I reply, my voice more neutral than I thought it would be. We both seem to just stare at each other, both of us needing to say something, anything, but we don't. We can't.

"Let's get on with this dinner, you are fifty minutes late already, Mackenzie. The poor cooks have been keeping the food warm the whole time," my father scolds me.

"Miss Crowe has an issue with being on time, it's something you should grow to expect from her, Alaric," Mr Daniels says, making me glare at him as I follow my father through the door that Mr Daniels holds open. When I pass Mr Daniels, his fingers graze down my back slowly, making me shiver and look behind me to see him smirking at me.

"Oh, she did turn up then, it's not like we've been waiting for ages," I hear Verity's whiny voice say. I look over to see her sitting at the table, a smug grin on her face as she turns to pointedly look to her left. I follow her gaze to see Enzo sitting next to her, holding her hand on the table. Anger and fury burns through my mind, and only Enzo's little shake of his head makes me calm down. I have to remind myself that he wouldn't really be dating her. That this must be a part of the plan or something, but it doesn't stop how much it hurts. Or how much I want to pick the knife up from the table and stab them both with it. Repeatedly.

"Hello, Verity, Enzo." I smile tightly, walking towards the seat opposite Enzo that my father holds out for me. As I sit, I can't help but trail my eyes over Enzo in his suit, reluctantly noting how fucking good he looks.

"You shouldn't stare, it's rude," Enzo says and I laugh.

"It's rude to bring a girl on a date with another girl you've seen half-naked and kissed, and yet here we are. All together," I say, laughing more when

Verity glares at me. I look away as Mr Daniels sits next to me and places his hand on my knee under the table, squeezing once. My father sits at the head of the table, and lifts a glass. I look around at the expensive looking table, the gold plates and crystal glasses. The large fireplace and paintings in the room. It's clear my father likes to live in luxury, like a king or something.

"A toast," he pauses as everyone picks up their glass. I watch his calculating eyes as they look around the table, pausing on how close Mr Daniels is to me and then back up to my eyes as he starts talking. *Why do I feel like I'm a mouse in his trap?*

"To our families, to changing this world for the better, and to Mackenzie. Who is the only one that can make all this happen," he toasts and everyone drinks from their glass, as I lock eyes with my father and put my drink down. *I'm not toasting to that.*

"How can I make what happen?" I ask, and he chuckles.

"I will tell you what your twelfth power is, if you do something for me," he offers, and I tilt my head to the side.

"What?" I ask, curious as to what he would want.

"You let my scientists and doctors examine you, test your powers."

"No, that could be dangerous for Mackenzie and everyone here," Mr Daniels snaps, his grip on my leg is borderline painful as it tightens on my knee.

"Would they hurt me?" I ask, curious to see him lie straight to my face once again.

"No, not at all. We just want to learn about you," my father answers, keeping eye contact with me the whole time and ignoring Mr Daniels completely. *He's a good liar, I will give him that.*

"Fine. One week of testing and you tell me what my twelfth power is," I reply, and look over to see Mr Daniels giving me a look that suggests I should stop talking.

"I love how demanding you are, just like your mother," he answers, not exactly agreeing with me.

"I want you to promise me, and don't speak about my mother," I snap and he laughs under his breath, leaning back in his seat.

"I promise to show you exactly what your twelfth power is in one week, Mackenzie. Now, we should eat," he says, clapping his hands, and the door to the right is opened as people start carrying food in. They place the plates between us, with roast chicken and a mixture of vegetables. I pile some food on my plate at the same time everyone else does, and we all start eating in silence.

"So, it's Enzo, correct?" my father asks.

"Yes," Enzo replies, looking over at my father.

"I have brought Verity up, like a daughter if you will. I hope you will treat her right," he says, making me tighten my grip on my fork.

"I was only invited for dinner, this isn't a date," Enzo replies coldly, and I hold back a smirk when Verity's face drops. "What a shame, I had such high hopes. With your eleven marks and Verity's ten, you'd be such a good match," Alaric says. I look between Enzo and him curiously.

"What do you mean by that?" I ask, and he smiles thinly at me.

"Well, here we believe that those with more power should look to partner with someone else who has a similar level of power. To ensure a pure next generation for us all," he explains plainly, and I feel my stomach twist. *He can't be serious?* Enzo coughs, looking severely uncomfortable, and Verity has a determined look on her face. *I really don't like that look.*

"That sounds... interesting," I manage to force out. There's a moment of awkward silence.

"Well, this food is fantastic," Mr Daniels says, breaking the silence. I turn my head to look at him, grateful for the subject change. It occurs to me how weird it is that I don't know his first name, and yet I feel so close to him. I squeeze his hand under the table, and make a mental note to ask next time I see him. It doesn't help that everyone either calls him Mr Daniels or just Daniels, meaning I haven't been able to catch it from anyone else either.

"Yes, it's delicious," Verity says, and I turn my head in her direction. She's not looking at the food. I feel my hands clench, and Mr Daniels uncurls the one he's holding, and rubs the palm of my hand with his thumb soothingly. Looking down, I take a deep breath.

"Personally, I think it's a little tasteless," Enzo remarks, making me look up. His dark eyes lock with mine, and I flash a grateful smile at him.

"Children, please play nicely," Alaric remarks in a humorous tone.

"This is nicely, I mean, nobody's been set on fire yet. That's what you like to do when things don't go your way, isn't it, Kenzie? Just go around setting people on fire? Like a little toddler having a tantrum," Verity says, narrowing her green eyes on me.

"Fuck you," I say plainly, over this whole polite dinner pretence. I'm so done with this dinner, done with this whole damn day. I stand, pushing my chair back, and dropping Mr Daniels' hand. His sister is a freaking nightmare.

"Going somewhere, Mackenzie?" Alaric asks.

"Yes, I'm going anywhere that bitch isn't," I snap, already walking out the room.

"Mackenzie, don't act so childish. Come back here and finish your dinner," he calls after me.

"Go to hell, daddy-dearest," I call over my shoulder sarcastically, leaving the room and that hellish dinner behind me. I walk quickly from the property, noticing all the guards along the perimeter wall, as I head back towards the main building where my room is located.

"Crowe, wait up!" Enzo's voice shouts from behind me. I turn to see him running in my direction.

"What are you doing here?" I question, slowing down slightly.

"I came to see if you were okay... and to escape the psycho bunny boiler, but mainly to make sure you're okay," he says, flashing me a grin. I try not to return the smile, but fail.

"I'm fine. I just needed to get out of there

80

before I really did set her on fire. I can't believe she's Mr Daniels' sister, they're so different."

"She was always a little evil and out of control, but coming here really changed her. Your father changed her," he says, reaching for my hand and pulling me to stop.

"So you're saying it's his fault, and she's a victim?" I ask, raising an eyebrow at him in question.

"Definitely not, I'm just telling you how she got the way she is. No matter what she's done, she's still his sister, and he wants to save her. Don't tell me you wouldn't do the same thing for Ryan," Enzo whispers.

"Ryan can still be saved, I know he can. He's not bad inside, but that woman is. She's got issues of the major kind, Enzo. They're not comparable."

"I think they're more alike than you'd care to admit," he comments.

"They're not. At least, I hope they aren't," I reply tightly. He wraps an arm around my waist and pulls me close.

"How about we take your mind off her and your brother for a little while?" he suggests in a low voice, making me shiver.

"What did you have in mind?" I ask, feeling a little breathless.

"Something a little like this..." he trails off, leaning down and locking his lips with mine. His hands grip my waist tightly as he kisses me, and he bites my lower lip, making me gasp from the shock of the sensation. He deepens the kiss, our tongues intertwining as he holds me close to him, and when he pulls away, I wish he didn't.

"I better stop now, before I can't," he whispers begrudgingly.

"What if I don't want you to?" the words slip out of my mouth before I can stop them.

"Well, then I'd at least suggest we find somewhere more private," he teases, gesturing around us, to the fact that we're in the middle of the open space in the compound, and there are guards watching us. I feel the heat creep into my cheeks.

"Yeah, maybe not right here," I reply, choking out a laugh.

"I have a surprise for you anyway, come with me," he says, tugging me with him. I follow after him, and he leads me to the block where I know East is being kept. He scans an access card on the door. An access card that certainly doesn't have his name.

"You stole that?" I ask quietly, not wanting to be overheard.

"I borrowed it. There's definitely a difference," he says lightly, making me laugh.

"Sure there is, thank you," I say, giving him a quick kiss.

"I figured you'd like to see East without the feeling of eyes watching you. They're so sure of the main grounds' security, there's nobody in here watching him at night. Just need the right access to get in and out. They figure even if he did manage to somehow escape this building, he'd never make it past the outside wall."

"Seems a little stupid to me," I comment as we walk down the corridor.

"It is. That's why Daniels suggested it," Enzo says, grinning. We stop outside the door and Enzo scans the card, unlocking it as the light flashes green. He hands me the card and turns away.

"Aren't you coming in?" I ask him, and he shakes his head.

"No, I thought you guys would like some privacy. I'll need that card back in the morning though, and you need to leave here before 6am, 5:30 to be extra careful," he says. I nod and head for the door to East's cell. I pause and turn back to Enzo.

"Thank you, you didn't have to do this," I say.

"I know, but I also know it would make you happy, Crowe, and I've decided I like how happy looks on you," he smiles, none of his usual sarcasm or snark is in his tone.

I give him one last smile, and push open the door to the cell, stepping in and closing it behind me.

# Chapter 9

MACKENZIE

"*K*enzie," East says, clearly surprised, as I walk across the room to him.

"Hey, East," I say quietly, as I pause standing by the bed. His eyes travel down me from head to toe and back up again, lingering on some places more than others.

"You look amazing, that dress is... wow," he mutters, standing up and pulling me to him, his hands resting firmly on my hips.

"This old thing?" I comment sarcastically. "Well, you always look '*wow*', so I just had to somehow compare for once," I say, smirking at him, feeling happy at the effect my appearance is having on him.

"Compare? You always outshine me, Kenz," he whispers.

"So fucking corny," I mutter.

"Only for you," he says, winking at me and making me laugh. He rests a hand on my cheek. "How did I miss how fucking amazing you are for so long? How could I have ever just thought of you as Ryan's little sister?" he asks.

"I don't know. I never thought of you as just Ryan's best friend," I admit, moving my hands up his shirt and running them across his toned stomach.

"Fuck, I think this is way too much talk about your brother," he growls, leaning down and kissing my jawline, and down to my neck. I moan as his lips find the sweet spot between my neck and shoulder, that damn spot is the undoing of me. I don't know how he knows it, but he does, nipping it with his teeth.

"I agree," I breathe, unbuttoning his shirt. His shirt falls to the ground, and I run my hands over his muscular chest and down his toned abs.

"We can stop now, you just need to tell me," East grounds out as my hand slides over his jeans and I stroke his hardness through the material.

"No, I don't want to stop. I've wanted you for as

long as I can remember and I—" I stop when I realise what I was just going to say, and that it could ruin the moment between us if he doesn't feel the same way. East grabs my head with both his hands, looking into my eyes like there is nothing else in the entire world.

"I love you too," he whispers and then he kisses me. I slide my hands into his hair as we battle for every demanding kiss, both of us desperate for each other. East takes his time sliding down the zip on the back of my dress as we kiss, brushing his fingers down my spine as he goes, and making me shiver from the sensation.

"Cold?" he whispers next to my ear, as he pushes the dress down my shoulders, letting it fall to the ground. East's eyes widen as he stares down at me, completely naked in front of him. The dress I wore was so tight I couldn't put any underwear on, but I don't hide from him. I trust East completely. Something snaps in East as he pulls me to him and starts kissing me again, and I kiss him back with just as much passion.

"No, I'm not cold," I manage to get out when he kisses down my neck, taking his time to find that sweet spot once more and sucking gently on it, sending me crazy with need for him. He picks me up suddenly, carrying me to the bed and placing me down on it. East lowers himself on top of me, and I slide my hands down his chest to undo his jeans.

"Are you on protection, Kenz?" he stops kissing me to ask.

"Yes," I reply, and he smirks as he crawls down my body. I moan loudly in pleasure as his lips find my right nipple and he flicks his tongue against the hard nub. His other hand slides down my stomach slowly, to tease me, before he cups me. He slides a finger slowly across my slit, teasing me with every slow movement as he watches me for my reaction.

"Fuck, Kenz, you're so wet," he groans as he slides a finger inside me and I can't help the moan that slips from my lips. His thumb goes to my clit at the same time, rubbing circles as his finger slides in and out of me in perfect rhythm. In a way, I hate that he's so good at this, but the other part of me doesn't care anymore. Not when he is with me now.

"So close," I whisper when the pleasure is getting too much and I'm inches away from coming. He moves his hand away, kissing me before sliding off me. East sits up on the bed, pulling me into his lap and pushing his jeans down. He slides a hand to the back of my neck and pulls me closer to him.

"I love you," I say as I hold myself above him,

just the tip of him inside me, before sinking down on top of him and kissing him before he can reply. I move my hips slowly at first, getting used to the size of him, but as our pleasure builds, we both lose ourselves quickly. East pushes me down onto the bed, lying on top of me, and thrusting into me hard and fast.

"Come for me, I want to feel you come on my cock, Kenz," East whispers in my ear, his seductive tone making me lose all of the control I was holding onto, and I feel myself tightening around him as I come.

"Kenz," East shouts as he finishes inside me, slowly thrusting as he calms down, resting his forehead on mine.

"Whatever happens, I'm yours, just know that," he tells me, and then kisses me gently. East rolls off me, pulling a blanket over us, and I lie facing him.

"And I'm yours, that is never changing, East," I tell him before kissing him. "We have all night, any suggestions for what else we could do?" I ask, not so innocently.

"Don't think I'm finished with you yet, Mackenzie Crowe," East chuckles as he rolls on top of me and kisses me, cutting me off before I can reply.

# Chapter 10

MACKENZIE

"**C**ome back soon, but only if it's safe," East asks me as I stand at the door, and smooth the creases out of my dress. I lean up, kissing him.

"I wish I didn't have to leave," I tell him honestly.

"You need to get back before sunrise," he says, but he doesn't look happy about it either. All I want to do is get back into bed, and repeat what we have been doing for the last few hours. I press a quick, final kiss to his lips.

"Go, before I decide that I can't let you," East says, letting me go as I open the door. I look around, seeing the empty hallway before closing it quietly behind me. I walk down the hallway and towards my room, only seeing a few guards around on my way there.

"Kenzie!" I hear Kelly shout behind me, and I turn to see her walking out from a room. She has a white coat on and she is holding a clipboard against her chest. I wait for her to catch up with me, and she pulls me into a hug.

"A little early for you, isn't it?" I ask her.

"I could say the same thing," she replies as she pulls away. "Come on, I'll walk back with you. I've been up all night in the lab," she adds.

"Lab?" I ask her as we walk.

"I heard someone was being brought in for testing, and that they will need a good healer if anything goes wrong, so I volunteered to train with the scientists," she says, shrugging her shoulders. I'm frightened about these tests, but it's good to know that I will have Kelly with me.

"For me, you did that for me?" I ask her and she tucks some of her blonde hair behind her ear before she answers.

"Yes," she replies simply, and I look over at her, seeing her bright, blue eyes watching me with love and a tiny bit of fear. I guess it's the fear of losing each other, that all those years of friendship are gone because of everything that happened. I know she feels guilty, I can see it, but I'm still mad.

"I hate that you lied to me, that you never told me you loved my brother. That you knew Ryan killed Mr Layan, that you kept so much from me and you were a shitty best friend recently," I bite out and I come to a stop in the corridor, crossing my arms. Kelly looks down at the ground, tears already falling from her eyes.

"I was a shitty friend, I know that. I should have trusted you, but I thought I was protecting you and Ryan. I never meant for things to get so out of control, I never knew how involved Ryan is," she sobs, "I thought I could convince him not to listen to his father and Verity, but..." she whispers the end part and can't say anymore, the words just trailing off. I pull her to me, wrapping my arms around her as she cries, and I find myself wiping a few tears away too.

"What happened to hoes before bros?" I joke lamely, thinking of the promise we made not to put boys before our friendship when we were ten. Although, I never expected that the boy causing the problems would by my brother.

"I forgot our promise we made," she laughs, "Where have you been anyway?" she asks, looking down at the dress I'm wearing, and giving a pointed look at my messy hair.

"I went to see East," I admit, and she raises an eyebrow at me.

"And?" she asks, dragging the word out. I bite my lower lip and her jaw drops. "You totally slept with sexy East didn't you? Wasn't that one of your life goals?" she asks, sounding both amused and impressed that I could now check off one of my items.

"Yeah, when I was like, thirteen. Gods, I can't believe I actually put that on my list," I say laughing as I remember the dumb lists we made. Kelly's things were all practical and sensible, and mine were well... I wanted East, ten dogs, and all the pizza the world has to offer. I frown when I notice that Kelly's smile has already dropped.

"Do you forgive me? Can you?" she asks more seriously, pulling away and I look at her. I would never have understood it, if it wasn't exactly what I'm trying to do now. I'm trying to convince Ryan myself, trying to save him and everyone I love. I get what she did, and Kelly isn't a bad person. I don't think she has a bad bone in her body. She made a mistake, but everyone does.

"I forgive you," I say, grabbing her hands and

then she starts to glow white, her eyes rolling back seconds before I'm pulled into her vision.

*"FORGIVE ME," a voice says but I can't hear him properly over the sound of rain, smashing rocks, and water splashing loudly in my ears. I blink my eyes open, seeing myself kneeling on the floor in a white dress, blood splattered all over it. Floating rocks are flying around me, rain is pouring from the skies, and a blue light is shining from the left of us, making it hard to see myself in the clearing. I'm holding a man in my arms, but I can only see his chest and legs. There is a dagger in his stomach, and my hand is covering it, glowing white.*

*"There's nothing to forgive, just don't die, okay? I love you, so you can't die," I reply, but I can't hear what the man says back as everything blurs, and my eyes are forced into closing before I know who it is.*

MY EYES FLY OPEN, and I release Kelly as if she burns, stumbling back from her. "What the hell was that? Who was it, did you see his face?" I question her, needing to know. It's obviously someone I care about. She shakes her head, the tears from before still filling her eyes.

"I didn't see his face, but I felt your pain, Kenzie. You were in so much pain," she chokes out, her entire body trembling.

I pull her back to me, wrapping my arms around her tightly. Whatever she just saw, we need to prevent. I have to believe that we saw that for a reason, that fate was giving us a chance to stop this from happening. "I need you to try and see more, Kelly," I say gently, and she pulls away.

"I can't. Kenzie, that hurt so much, your heart, I swear it broke," she whispers.

"Please, Kelly, I wouldn't ask if it wasn't important. We need to at least try and find out who it is, so we can stop this," I insist. More tears trail down her face.

"Some things can't be changed, Kenz, you know that. Some visions feel concrete, completely set in stone. Others feel ever-changing, and just a possible route the path could take us..." she trails off, shaking harder. She swallows thickly and looks me straight in the eyes. "I'm so sorry, that one feels definite. I've never had a vision feel so concrete."

"I won't accept that, I can't. It's not happening!" I snap, turning away.

"Kenzie!" Kelly shouts after me.

"Leave me alone, I need to figure this out, Kells.

If you won't help me, I'll try and bring on the vision myself," I say, walking away as quickly as I can. I won't accept this. This isn't happening. It had to be one of the guys in that vision, and I refuse to lose any of them. I freeze. *Fuck, what if it was East?* My heart couldn't take it if it was him. I may be falling for the others, but East has had my heart for as long as I can remember. I take a deep breath, and carry on walking back to my room. I need to get my shit together and figure this out, before I lose one of them for real.

# Chapter 11

MACKENZIE

*G*ritting my teeth and trying for the millionth time, I call on my divination mark, picturing the eye with the swirls, while also trying to focus on the vision Kelly had before. Finally, I feel a vision pull me in.

*"WHERE THE HELL ARE WE?" I ask, looking around. The landscape around me is unfamiliar, and feels so different to anywhere I have been before. The whole place seems to pulse with the magic of our marks.*

*"I can't believe it. We're really here," Enzo's voice replies, as he pulls me close. He sounds so amazed, so in awe of this place, and I am too. It's all real.*

*"I'm so fucking glad you're here with me," I whisper, leaning up and kissing him...*

"WHAT ARE YOU DOING?" Locke asks from the doorway, pulling me from my vision. I quickly open my eyes and look at him, trying to force a smile onto my face.

"Nothing, just um, meditating?" I say, shrugging and feigning nonchalance. I can't help but feel disappointed, I finally bring on a vision and it's the wrong one.

"You don't seem like the meditating type," he replies with a smirk, as he steps into the room and shuts the door behind him.

"I'm trying to bring on a vision, I want to try and see if I can work out what Alaric is planning," I say, giving him a half-truth at least. I don't want to worry him about Kelly's vision. I don't want to worry any of them, or burden them with this, not yet anyway. I'll find out who it is in the vision first, I'll figure out how to stop this, and then I'd tell them.

"Wouldn't Kelly be better for this job? No offence to your divination mark powers, but Kelly is an extremely powerful seer from what I've heard. Plus, I wouldn't put too much trust in visions, Kenz. You know nothing is foolproof with them, you can't trust them to always show you the truth," he says, taking a seat on the bed next to me. I launch myself at him, wrapping my arms around him tightly. "Woah, Kenzie, what's this for?" he asks, cuddling me back.

"I just really needed to hear that right now, Locke. You wouldn't believe how much," I whisper, squeezing him tightly.

"What's wrong?" he asks, stroking my hair and pulling me onto his lap.

"I don't want to talk about it, and plus, I don't even have time right now," I say. I let myself relax for a moment against his chest, just listening to the repeated rhythm of his heartbeat.

"Why don't you have time?"

"I have to leave for testing in like..." I trail off, looking for the clock on the wall. "Ten minutes ago," I finish, seeing the time. I groan and reluctantly pull myself away.

"Nope, not so quick," he says, pulling me back and pressing his lips firmly to mine. I sigh in contentment, and then kiss him again, wrapping my arms around his neck and straddling his lap. His hands move down over my ass, tugging me closer to him.

A cough from the door makes me freeze. "Mackenzie, you're meant to be in the lab," Alaric calls from the door. I roll my eyes. Great, because being tested on like a freaking lab rat is what I want to be doing right now, as if. I look at Locke, his hair is all ruffled and he looks sexy as hell. *Yeah, I could think of better things to be doing right now.*

"Mackenzie," he calls again impatiently.

Standing up, I make a huffing noise as I follow him from the room. As I reach the door, giving one last look and quick smile to Locke before I turn back and leave, heading for the stupid lab.

---

"JUST TRY AND KEEP CALM," the man in the white coat says.

"Keep calm? You're planning on using the pain mark on me while I'm covered in freaking suckers on my head, and a million monitors beeping around us. You want me to keep calm? Are you fucking insane?" I seethe.

"We just want to see if the mark will attempt to

trigger, and what happens to your brainwaves and heart rate if that occurs," he explains.

"Oh, and that makes it all okay then," I snap.

"Please relax, Miss Crowe," the man tells me, and then he presses his hand down on my shoulder. Pain shoots through my body instantly, my teeth clamp down and the sound of beeping filling the room is the only thing I can focus on for a second. The beeping gets louder, as I try to focus through the pain he is dishing out. Try and keep calm my ass. He either isn't using all his power on me, or is very weak with the pain mark as it doesn't hurt that bad I am eventually able to think. Not bad enough to make my other marks want to fight him. It's only annoying, like little bugs prickling all over my skin.

"Enough, this will not work. Emotions trigger the twelfth mark, and I finally found proof in the things stolen from the academy," a woman says as she walks into the room. The man moves his hand away and I take a deep breath. I roll to the side to see Kelly walking in, and she runs over to me, placing her hands on my head. They light up, warming my forehead and side of my face where she touches, making me instantly start to feel better. I sit up, pulling all the wires off me before looking back at the woman who watches me. She has long black hair tied up, a white coat on, and she holds an old looking book in her hands. I pick up my jumper from the end of the bed and pull it over my head.

"Can I show you something, Mackenzie?" she asks me when I'm done and I nod, sliding off the table.

"Whatever you have to show me can't be any fucking worse than that," I reply and follow her over to a table. She sits down, and I take the seat next to her as she opens the book. It's old enough to be falling apart, the pages are torn at the ends and crumbling as she moves them. The woman opens the book to the last page, where the twelfth mark is in the middle. There are people drawn all around it, and the arrow is bigger, dividing the sphere and the people. I look down it, knowing this little mark is the cause of all the trouble in this world. One tiny mark. I look underneath the mark to see the rows and rows of symbols written in a paragraph.

"They're Ariziadian markings, or how they write. We don't know the real name. That's what is written underneath, as this book is from Ariziadia," she tells me.

"The rumoured place all marked come from? The old fairy tale that our parents used to tell us, to scare us into going to sleep? Go to sleep or you might fall through a portal to Ariziadia," Kelly asks with a slight laugh, as she sits in the seat next to me. We have all heard the fairy tales of Ariziadia. That it's another world, where marked originals came from, but it's only rumours used to make marked children go to bed. Just like humans have their fairy tales of the big bad wolf. There is nothing of real proof anymore, nothing to prove the world ever existed all those millions of years ago. Even the books, the water in the academy, and every artefact can be explained away as things ancient marked made in *this world*. Not brought over from Ariziadia.

"It's not rumoured, it's real, and the council have always known this. This book is from there, as are many other things we have collected," the woman snaps and looks worried when I raise my eyebrows at her.

"I wouldn't speak to my friend like that, not if you want my help," I say, watching as she looks at me and then back to Kelly.

"I'm sorry, I've spent my whole life researching a place you just claimed is rumoured, please under-stand," she says to Kelly, who nods.

"So...can you read this?" I ask, placing my finger on the symbols. They look like marks, just smaller and every one of them is different from any marks we know.

"Yes. This claims that the twelfth power is drawn out by emotion, heavy emotion. Be it fear, sorrow or love," she says, tracing a finger over the book in almost a loving motion. I bet this woman is married to her work.

"Well there's nothing we can do here then," I say. Wanting to leave and maybe break into this woman's room later to find out what the twelfth mark is myself.

"I believe we should test this new theory with your friend Kelly...and me," Verity says, as she walks into the room like she owns it. Dressed in all leather again, and her stupid shiny hair looks good as it moves around her. Gods how much I want to be petty as fuck, and cut all her hair off in her sleep.

"I don't believe that it would be smart to test such high emotions at this time," the woman shakes her head and gets up, "I will go and ask Mr Daniels or Alaric what their opinion is on the matter, with this new information," she says, practically running out the room after grabbing the book. Looks like I'm not the only one who wants to move very quickly in the other direction whenever Verity shows up.

"Let's go," I tell Kelly, standing up as Verity moves in front of me.

"Everyone out, now," Verity shouts, and I watch in the corner of my eye as all the scientists and healers run out from the room. *This can't be good.*

"What are you doing? Your brother wouldn't let you do this. You've already had a warning, and the next time your brother won't be able to protect you from getting locked up. Playing the innocent sister won't work forever, as fucked up as you are," Kelly spits out. Verity steps back and slams all the doors in the room shut with her air power.

"No one will hate me for activating the twelfth power. You should be thankful Kelly, you have no idea what Kennie's daddy dearest has planned for her," she chuckles, and I grab Kelly's arm when she steps forward. While I'm distracted stopping Kelly from attacking the crazy bitch, she lifts her hands into the air and then pulls them down, making me and Kelly slam onto the floor.

"What happens when the twelve and her friend run out of air?" Verity chuckles, and aims her hands at us both. I go to call my powers when I realise I can't breathe, and I panic. I roll on the floor, feeling my lungs being strangled and black dots slowly appear in front of my eyes the more I struggle to breathe.

"Maybe I should kill your friend? It would teach you a lesson for going after my Enzo, you little slut," she says, and the pressure increases in my chest. I scream in my head as I taste blood in my mouth, calling every single one of my marks. I turn my head to the side and see Kelly turning blue, her eyes wide and panicked as blood pours from the corner of her mouth. The twelfth power takes over as I stare at Kelly, burning the back of my neck as I close my eyes. I feel each one of my marks start to burn, the fire mark, the water mark...

"NO! You stupid girl, she will destroy the whole unit!" I hear Alaric scream, seconds before a hand punches me hard in the face, and everything goes black.

# Chapter 12

## MACKENZIE

*M*y dream is strange, blurred and yet clear. Loud and then silent. I'm aware that I'm dreaming, but I get so lost in it, it feels completely real.

I look around the table, seeing all my loved ones surrounding me, but something is missing. Someone is missing. We're all eating dinner, forcing smiles and laughing, but something is so wrong.

Someone's eyes are sad. Someone else is looking over at the door constantly, as if waiting for him to come in. My heart feels like it's shattered, and I don't know how I will ever heal fully. A hand links in mine, and I turn to face the man I've been in love with since we were kids. He squeezes my hand and lays a kiss on my forehead comfortingly.

"I love you, Kenzie. It'll get better, just give it time," he whispers. I feel the teardrops rolling down my face, I taste *them when they cross over my lips, the salty tang sticking to my tongue. Maybe he's right, but right now, it's not time to feel better. The wound is still too fresh, and it burns me deeply, cutting me straight to my core.*

*"I love you too, East," I whisper. I'm so relieved to have him and the others here today here to support me. I don't know what I'd have done if I'd lost them all. They kept me going through all the destruction my twelfth mark caused.*

*"I know you do," he says with a small smile. He runs a hand through his hair, looking every bit the picture of perfection. A warm hand rests on my shoulder and I turn around to face him.*

BLINKING OPEN MY EYES, I look up at the white ceiling for a moment, before immediately shutting them again. The light is way too bright.

"She's awake," an unfamiliar voice shouts loudly, hurting my ears.

"Can you keep it down," I grumble. A hand touches my shoulder, and I recoil away in pain. Noises are too loud. Lights are too bright. The slightest touch sets every nerve in my body on fire. Everything is too much. "Too much," I whisper.

"Get another healer in here. Get Kelly!" I hear a familiar voice demand. The demand is followed by muffled whispers. "No, I don't care if she's still recovering, Miss Crowe is in agony. She will come in here and help her," he growls. I can hear the absolute franticness in his tone. I've never heard Mr Daniels like that, not to this level. *He really does care...* I can't let him bring Kelly to help me, not when she's hurt.

"N-no," I mumble, trying to force my eyes open again, but my body won't follow orders, and my eyes stay shut. "Don't get Kelly," I manage to whisper, before passing out again.

# Chapter 13

## MR DANIELS

"*I* don't care what you have to do, you will make her fucking better. I don't care if you have to grab every fucking healer in this camp, you will do whatever it takes," I snap at the doctor who has been monitoring Kenzie. I haven't left her side since she passed out again half an hour ago. I'd debated going to get Kelly, but I didn't want to go against her wishes. Not unless I have to. If the other healers can't do the job, she will. Miss Crowe's wishes be damned.

"We are doing everything possible to ensure Miss Crowe's wellbeing, we just need some more time so we can heal her. We won't let anything happen to her," he says.

"Bullshit," I say, grinding it out between my

clenched teeth. *They won't let anything happen to her? They already have.* I knew we should have left yesterday, but no, we planned for tonight. Looking at Kenzie lying comatose on the bed, I know we won't be leaving tonight as planned. *Fuck. I need to call the council.* And now I know I need to get Verity out of here first. My body tenses as I think of my sister. She did this. She caused Kenzie this pain. Maybe what Kenzie saw at the school was true, but I don't want to believe my sister is completely gone. The good in her has to be there still. I would get her away from here, and in time, she would realise her mistakes. I just have to hope that Kenzie will forgive me for needing to save Verity too. My sister is all that is left of my family, and I don't intend to lose her too. Stroking a hand down the side of Kenzie's sleeping face, I'm lost in my thoughts.

Kenzie doesn't understand Verity like I do, she doesn't know what she has gone through, what happened to her as a child. I hold Kenzie's sleeping hand tighter as I remember what one of my fathers did, how he used the pain mark on her when she was only a toddler. I wish I could kill him, but my other dad did that for me, for all of us. I know she isn't evil inside, she was so sweet before it happened, but ever since then, the trauma changed her, the magic changed her. She manifested her pain mark before ever stepping into the waters at the academy, not that we ever revealed that to anyone outside of our family. The kind of attention that marked anomalies give you is always the bad kind.

A hand rests on my shoulder and I shrug it off. "Fuck off," I mutter.

"Cut the shit, Daniels. We're all worried about her," Enzo says, and then he leans down to whisper. "Get your crap together and play your part properly. He can't know how deeply you care for her, not for this to work," he whispers harshly, but I know he's right. Letting go of her hand, I swallow and stand up, heading for the doctor.

"You know we need her alive for what her mark does; if she dies, we have nothing. You fucking have her awake and healed by morning, or you'll never wake again. Do you understand me?" I snap. He nods frantically, and I swear I hear one of the twins chuckle. "Do you think this is funny?" I turn around, snapping at Locke. He points at Logan next to him. "You then, asshole, do you think this is funny?" I growl.

He narrows his eyes on me. "Of course it isn't funny, I'm worried as shit. What made me chuckle was Locke's comment about the doctor looking like he just shit his pants. You're a scary fucker, Daniels, to most people anyway," he replies. I let out a breath and grunt. *Maybe I did take it too far with the doctor?*

Looking at Kenzie one last time before I leave the room, I decide there isn't a '*too far*' here. I would do anything for her. I send off a silent prayer to whatever gods may be listening. *Please let her be okay.*

---

ONCE I AM FAR ENOUGH AWAY from the compound, I pull over on the side of the road and pull my burner phone out. I dial my contact at the council.

"I need to speak to Mrs Curwood, now. It's important," I snap as soon as he answers.

"Nice to talk to you too, Daniels," Miles' voice responds sarcastically.

"No fucking time, transfer me now," I snap.

"You're always such a pleasure," he snaps back, and then before I can reply, I hear the transfer hold music. Who *fucking thought people waiting on hold would want to listen to this crap?* I almost smash my phone to escape the awkward 90s music. Like anyone wants a reminder of that.

"You have news?" Mrs Curwood's voice comes down the phone.

"Kenzie and Kelly are injured. They're with healers and should be okay, but we cannot do the move tonight. It's off. Call it all off," I say quickly.

"Call it all off? Our team is already in position, and ready to go on your signal. We have been planning this since she was taken, and now you are telling me we have to put this off?" she replies. I grip my steering wheel with my free hand tightly.

"Did you miss the part where I said both Kenzie, and your daughter Kelly are injured?" I say, hoping she meant to say something

"Surely we can pull this off, even if they are injured," she says plainly.

"They're not in a fit state to travel. I'm telling you it can't be done," I growl. "Are you not the least concerned about your daughter?" I snap.

"I'm sure Kelly will be fine, as you said, she is being looked after by healers, is she not?" she replies, and I grit my teeth to keep in the reply. That woman is an emotionless robot. I've hated her from the moment I'd met her at the council building in London last year. She cares only about results, never what it takes to achieve those results. I wasn't surprised when she had so easily agreed to allow her untrained daughter to take part in such a dangerous mission, but this is a whole new level of low. *How can someone be so uncaring towards their family? Does she not realise how lucky she is?*

"Daniels, are you still there?" she asks.

"Here, but I'm going. Don't send them in under any circumstances. Trust me, if you attack without my help from inside, you will fail. I'll call tomorrow." I hang up the phone before she can reply, and then I roughly throw it at the windscreen. I cringe when I see the chip it's caused there. *Fuck, that's gonna spread.* I'll be avoiding potholes like my life depends on it.

I get out of the car, slamming the door behind me and just walk for a bit, stretching my legs. So much adrenaline is coursing through me, I need an outlet, I need to do something. I call my protection mark, and then I call forth my wolf, shifting easily. A quick run in this form should do the trick nicely.

## Chapter 14

MACKENZIE

"Enzo?" I ask, hearing him talking to me, or maybe he's talking to someone else, but everything is blurry as I just about croak out his name.

"Take it easy, I'm here, Crowe," he says, his voice soothing as I feel a finger tuck a piece of my hair behind my ear as I blink my eyes open. The room is bright with the artificial lights on the ceiling, and everything looks so white. From the white walls to the white sheets I'm tucked into.

"What happened?" I ask, turning my head to the side of the bed where Enzo is sitting watching me. He looks worn out, with big dark bags under his eyes, his hair looks like someone has rubbed their fingers through it a million times and his clothes are wrinkled.

"Do you not remember?" he asks me, taking my hand in his and squeezing tightly as everything comes back to me in fast flashes. Verity using her air mark on me and Kelly. Kelly's face turning blue, her eyes panicked, the feeling of suffocating.

"You're okay, relax, Crowe," Enzo says, but I can't stop thinking about the pain. The feeling of being so desperate to live, the twelfth power taking over without me calling it and how it burned each one of my marks. It hurt so much, my marks still feel sore from it as I feel them on my body. Enzo leans over me, pulling my head to face him and kisses me. I'm in shock for a second as he moves his lips against my own frozen ones, before I relax into the sweet kiss and return it.

"Get out of that head and be with me, Crowe. I will keep you safe, I'm never going to let you down again," he promises me when he stops the kiss, but he keeps his lips close to mine. Our eyes are locked together and I feel, the promise in them. I feel everything as I stare at him, the emotion, the pain of nearly losing me, the anger and something else I can't even think of. Let alone say out loud, so I just stare into his dark eyes, wanting to get lost in the darkness of them.

"Enzo," I whisper and he grins.

"So speechless that you can only say my name? I like that look on you," he grins and makes me chuckle a little as he pulls away, but stays by my side. He pulls his phone out, texting away as I begin to ask questions.

"Where is Kelly, is she okay?"

"Recovering still, but awake and demanding to see you," he says, "Ryan has practically locked her in the room until the healers say it's safe for her to get up." I smile at the idea of anyone stopping Kelly from seeing me, much like I want to see her, and would if every part of my body didn't hurt. I actually don't think I could get up off the bed without face planting the floor.

"And Verity?" I ask, hoping that she hasn't just gotten away with it. Enzo's face clouds over in anger as he spits out.

"Locked up, and she won't be getting out anytime soon."

"Miss Crowe," Mr Daniels breathes out in relief when he slams into the room. He doesn't look any better than Enzo does, with his rumpled clothes and pale face. His hair is messy, but it's still a sexy mess, and he doesn't move as he stares at me.

"Mr Daniels," I say softly, and Enzo looks between us before standing up. Enzo leans over me, kissing me lightly before whispering.

"I'm going to find you some food and you two should get rid of all the secrets. Talk about why he protects Verity," he says, shocking me into silence. He leans away and walks out the room, patting Mr Daniels' shoulder and the two of them seem to have some kind of silent conversation. Mr Daniels shuts the door behind Enzo and walks over to me as I pull myself up on the bed a little.

"Do you want a drink, Miss Crowe?" he asks me and I nod.

"I asked you to call me Kenzie," I say as I watch him pour me a glass of water and bring it over, sitting on the edge of the bed.

"I remember, I don't think I will ever forget when you asked me that," he says as I take a deep drink, and then place the glass on the side.

"How are you feeling?" he asks me, his green eyes seem to be accessing my every move.

"Honestly, a little sore, but I'm more worried about Kelly, and I'm feeling like I never want to see Verity again or I'm going to try and kill her," I tell him honestly, and he looks down at the ground. I expected him to argue with me, try and convince me she's all rainbows and sunshine but he doesn't.

"Did you know we had two dads? I believe Verity is my half-sister, but as you know in our world, that means very little," he tells me.

"Same with me and Ryan, I don't think he is Alaric's son. He has my other dad's eyes, and he doesn't look much like me or him," I reply.

"I agree," Mr Daniels replies.

"You're still trying to save your sister, aren't you?" I ask him.

"I'm trying to save the little girl I remember. The girl who played with dolls, who loved dogs, and who I used to watch movies with every Sunday after dinner," he replies sadly.

"That isn't her anymore," I say gently. "She isn't that sweet girl, she's pure evil now."

"I know," he says, and I reach up to place my hand on his arm. He catches it, bringing it to his lips, and kissing the back of it slowly before looking up at me.

"At some point, I realised I had lost her, but I still couldn't admit it to myself. I just kept repeating the same thing in my head, that she will choose to be good in the end. That she won't betray me...but then she hurt you. The woman she knows how much I fucking care about...and she still did that. Even if you were a stranger, she shouldn't have done that," he says angrily, and kissing my hand once more.

"She didn't care when she hurt me and Kelly, she liked the power," I tell him, remembering the look in her eyes.

"I didn't know how far gone she was until I saw you in here, and her smiling when I visited her just now. She isn't sorry, not one part of her is," he says.

"I'm sorry, and I'm sorry that you can't save her. Just like I don't know if I can save Ryan, I think Verity may have changed him too much," I admit, biting my lip.

"I'm losing everything, first my parents, now my sister and—" he starts to list but I lift my hand out of his and place a finger against his lips.

"You won't lose me," I say and move my hand as he goes to say something else, but the door is opened.

"Mackenzie, how good it is to see you awake," Alaric says as he walks into the room, pausing to look between me and Mr Daniels.

"Daniels, you are needed in room sixteen," he snaps out.

"Of course I am," he replies as he stands. He heads for the door and turns looking at me over his shoulder. "I will come see you later, *Kenzie.*"

"I'll see you later then," I reply, giving an awkward half-wave. Turning to Alaric I narrow my eyes. "What do you want?"

"Is that any way to greet your father, Mackenzie?" he asks.

"Not really, it's a good thing the three of them aren't here," I retort.

"None of them are your actual father though, are they?" he questions.

"They all are. Leave me alone," I snap.

"And here I was thinking you were finally coming around," he drawls, stepping around the bed to look at my chart.

"Well, almost being killed by your little psycho soldier doesn't exactly help your cause." I cross my arms and try to sit up straighter, not wanting to relax around him.

"Verity has overstepped and will be handled," he says plainly.

"Handled?" I echo questioningly.

"She has her talents, of course, but she is proving too much of a risk. There's really no other choice," he replies, as if it's obvious.

"You don't mean...?" I ask, trailing off, too horrified to finish the sentence.

"Well, we will have to make it appear an accident. Daniels wouldn't be pleased about little sister being removed. I have a plan that will take him away from the compound tonight in order to ensure it runs smoothly," he explains.

"Why are you telling me this?" I ask, dumbfounded.

"Because you have no love for that girl, I'm sure. And I need to assure you that your safety is paramount to all of us here." I can't keep in the laugh at that comment. "Something funny, Mackenzie?"

"Yeah, that you think I'm stupid enough to believe any of this," I reply, rolling my eyes.

"Well, when Verity is gone tomorrow, then you will believe," he says firmly, crossing the room back to the door.

"Going so soon?" I call sarcastically.

"I will check in on you later, Mackenzie," he calls back as he leaves.

# Chapter 15

MACKENZIE

*S*taring up at the ceiling of my room here, I feel sick to my stomach. They moved me back into my room a few hours ago to rest, and as much as I try to forget my father's words and threat to Verity, I can't. I try to tell myself that she's evil and twisted, and that she deserves whatever she gets, but then I picture Mr Daniels' face when he finds out his sister is dead, and I can't do it. I can't just let it happen.

I force myself up off the bed, and dress into some plain clothes. I'm still weak from before, and even getting dressed tires me out. I push through the exhaustion and head to find Mr Daniels, hoping that I can get to him before he leaves. I realise that I have no idea where to find him. I have no idea where to find any of the guys, but I know where one person is at least. Luckily, I manage to navigate the corridors without much of an issue. I go to the only person whose room I know the location of, and knock on the door. After a nerve-wrecking moment where I worry he's not here, the door opens.

"Kennie," he says, his face shows how shocked he is to see me.

"Hey, Ry. Do you know where Mr Daniels is?" I ask.

"He just left on some weird job for our dad, why?" he questions, seeing the concern on my face. *Crap, I left it too long, and now he's not going to forgive me if he finds out I knew.* "Kennie, tell me what's wrong."

"He's going to kill Verity," I blurt.

"He's going to kill his sister?" he questions, confused.

"No, not Mr. Daniels, Alaric. He's going to kill her," I reply. Ryan grabs my arm and pulls me inside, slamming the door shut.

"Are you sure?" he asks frantically.

"Yes, he told me himself. He thought I would be happy about it!" I try to keep my breathing even. He seems to suddenly relax more, letting out a deep breath.

"She did hurt you, she almost killed you, maybe it's for the best?"

"Two wrongs don't make a right here, Ry. We can't just let this happen," I say.

"You're scared Daniels will blame you," he guesses.

"A little, but it's not right either way," I reply. "Please, help me."

"I'm not sure what we can do, break her out and escape? This place is a fortress."

"You must know something? Please, Ry. If there's some secret back exit somewhere here, or a spot on the guarded perimeter that isn't constantly monitored, then I really need to know where I can find it," I plead.

"No, there's no back exit, and no gap in security," he says, shaking his head. I groan in frustration, leaning my head against the wall. "Wait. There's always the tunnels," he breathes.

"Tunnels?"

"They run right under the compound for about a mile in a few different directions. They're meant to all be blocked, but I know that the south tunnel has a way through," he says.

"We need to get East too," I say quickly and he sighs.

"I knew you'd say that."

"Is that a no to helping me?"

"It's a begrudging yes. I have an idea, but you'll have to trust me, Kennie. I'm doing this to save her life and to free East. This doesn't change how I feel about the resistance, it doesn't change what side I'm on. But I don't want to see anyone hurt, especially not East. Verity, I'm not happy with right now, hell, I'm furious she hurt you, but she has been there for me this past year, so I can't let her die either. And I get why you can't, you're too good a person for that."

"Thank you," I whisper, pulling my brother into a tight hug.

"Yeah, yeah, let's see if you'll be thanking me when you hear the plan," he says dryly, as he pats my back.

---

"THIS BETTER WORK," I mutter, smelling the vodka I've spilt on my top. I keep going over and over the plan in my head, making sure we aren't missing anything. I walk towards the doors leading outside the compound that Ryan said is the least guarded. Ryan promises all the guards carry stun guns, not real ones, and all I have to do is get hold of one. I try to remember Mr Daniels, and how he would feel if Verity died tonight. I can't let that happen. I push the door open, seeing three of the six guards walking around stopping in their tracks to look at me.

"Hi, boys!" I say, wobbling a little on purpose as I slide out the door and it slams against the wall. "Whoops," I say loudly, followed by a laugh. I walk over to them slowly, pretending to stumble, and they hold their guns up in my direction. They all stand together in a tight circle as they watch me. Good, altogether just like I need them.

"Go and find one of her men or Daniels," one of the guards says to another two who run back into the building and shutting the door I left open. Dammit, I need all of them here.

"Miss Crowe, please go back inside," one of the braver guards says in a strict tone as he steps in front of the others.

"You remind me of my teacher," I do a fake giggle in between my words, "He would always be like "Miss Crowe, you're late. Miss Crowe, you shouldn't do that..." I trail off and burst into faked laughter. They lower their guns, looking at each other with confused expressions.

"But do you want to know a secret?" I say, stepping closer, trying to look like I'm almost tripping on my feet.

"Not particularly, Miss Crowe," the guard replies, and I snort as I laugh at him.

"Miss Crowe, you're clearly drunk. Why don't I escort you back to your room?" the brave guard says, stepping closer and I pretend to fall to the ground quickly. He catches me, dropping his stun gun to make sure I don't hurt myself. *Perfect.*

"What the hell did she drink?" the brave one says as I pretend to be out of it as he lowers me to the floor. "Because I want some. This shift was boring as hell until drunk girl turned up,".

"We should call Alaric," one replies in a serious tone, and I open my right eye slightly to see as I use my air power to pull the stun gun into my hand. I laugh when I jump up, shooting the brave one in front of me and jumping behind him as he falls, using his body as a shield as I shoot the others who are standing together and never see it coming. *Idiots.* I drop the guard onto the floor, looking around and seeing one other guard running away, looking back like he can sense me watching him. He raises his hands in surrender, but I lift my gun, shooting before he does anything. This isn't the time to feel sorry for the guards, they chose this and I didn't.

I pull my phone out, sending the message to Ryan to say it's all clear. I use my earth power to bury the guards in the ground, leaving little holes in the dirt so they can all still breathe. I run over to the door, flattening my body against it and holding the gun at my side.

*Come on, come on, come on, Ryan.* Finally, the door opens and I lift my gun, holding it up as Ryan steps out, followed by East and Verity, who still has handcuffs on her wrists. East pulls me to him, kissing me and letting go quickly.

"Damn, it's good to see you, Kenz," he says, linking our fingers as we start to run after Ryan, who is dragging Verity along towards the exit tunnels.

"Why?" Verity asks me as she slows down, so she is next to me.

"For Mr Daniels, so don't make me regret this. Next time I won't hold back. Why don't you be the sister he believes in and wants alive, instead of a class A bitch," I snap at her as we get to the high gate. I know we could try and fly over it with our mark, or East could literally fly if he shifted. Part of me wants to escape, but I know I can't, not with the twins, Kelly, Mr Daniels and Enzo still here. Plus, we could be spotted going over the wall. The tunnel plan was the safest, the hidden entrance is just a few more feet away.

"Once you're through, there's a car on the road with the keys in. Just get in it and follow the directions on the map I left in there. The people at the place I found will keep you safe," he tells East and Verity. East pulls me to him as Ryan undoes Verity's handcuffs. She shakes her wrists and starts laughing.

"You never know when you've been trapped and tricked, huh, Mackenzie?" Verity says and slams my brother into the barrier using her air mark, and he lands with a big thud.

"RYAN!" I shout as East turns, blocking me from Verity, and hitting her with a wave of water, slamming her into a tree.

"Shift and go," I pull at his shoulder, stepping in front of him as he looks down at me, "This cannot be for nothing. Go, East. I love you,".

"I can't leave you with her," he shakes his head.

"I can handle her, just go!" I scream at East, turning away from him as Verity gets up and runs at me. I don't look back at East as I lift my hands and fly into the air, calling my fire mark, throwing a fireball at her. She dodges as I make another one, and she flies into the air, the fireball hitting her arm, knocking her to the ground. I jump down, running to Ryan as I hear a squawk of a hawk in the distance sending relief flooding through me. East is free at least.

"Ry?" I shake his shoulder, seeing that he is bleeding from his head. I put my hands on his head to heal him, when a hand on my shoulder makes me scream. I look up to see Verity smiling down at me as she uses her pain mark, bringing me to my knees from the pain.

"Stop!" I scream out, trying to pull her hand off my shoulder and calling my protection mark, pushing it against her. I'm still in pain as I manage to turn my head to look at her, but it's not controlling me anymore.

"Why? Why do this to your brother? Why be like this?" I shout at her, seeing sweat dripping down her forehead as she smirks at me.

"I don't give a damn about my brother, he let my dad use the pain mark on me as a child. He left me with maids and a damn old nanny to go to the academy to learn about his powers. He chose you over the whole rebellion, over me!" she screeches.

"He never chose me," I reply, gritting my teeth together as I put my hand over hers and call my own pain mark, slamming it into her with everything I've got. She jumps away from me and we both stand, staring at each other as guards run over to us in the background.

"He chose you, I saw it the first time I saw him look at you. He loves you, he will give everything up, everything our parents worked and died for," she spits out, "All for a pretty girl."

"Maybe if you weren't so fucking crazy and jealous, you would see that your parents were wrong! You are wrong, Verity!" I shout at her as the guards surround us.

"Let's hope your dear daddy feels the same," she laughs, "Oh wait, he prefers me as a daughter anyway. You're just a tool we need alive for now, nothing more," she says and walks through the guards towards the building.

"Next time you try anything stupid, Mackenzie, I will kill you myself," she shouts back at me, as she disappears from my view and before I can say a word in return.

# Chapter 16

MACKENZIE

*S*itting on the cold floor of an unfamiliar grey room, I try to ignore the smug look on Verity's face as she looks down at me. The victory in her green eyes is clear; she tricked us, betrayed us, and now we were going to pay the price for it. *Great.*

"You really thought you could all just walk out of here?" Alaric asks me. I look to Ryan who is lying unconscious on the floor across from me.

"I can't believe she really believed she could just leap over the wall and into freedom," Verity snorts, and I freeze as I stare at her. *Wait, does she not know about the tunnels?*

"I wasn't going anywhere. I was trying to save you, you selfish bitch," I growl.

"Save me? Did you really believe he was going to kill me?" she taunts, leaning down over me, a smug grin spread across her face. Her eyes suddenly widen, and she chokes. I blink in confusion, then I see the blood, and the knife in her gut. We have so many powers that could do the job, so many kinder ways to do it, but Alaric stabs her with a knife. I look over her shoulder, and he's holding her from behind with his arm wrapped around her stomach, still holding the blade in. Verity's head turns slightly, as if trying to look at him, and her mouth moves, but no sound comes out. He drags the knife further up her stomach, before roughly pulling the blade out. He steps back and lets her drop to the floor.

"You're both fools," he says quietly, as he steps over her and towards me. I scramble back, trying to get away from both him and the blood that's seeping across the floor. He laughs.

"How could you just gut her like that?" I shout, and I flick my eyes behind him at Verity. I feel sick to my stomach when I see that she's still alive, but bleeding out fast. I doubt even a healer as gifted as Kelly could save her right now.

"Who else knew about your escape attempt?" he asks.

"Nobody," I answer honestly.

"You're saying Daniels has no idea you were attempting to break out his sister?" he questions disbelievingly.

"Do you really think he'd let us do it? You know if he knew what I had planned, he'd have done it himself," I reply, and he nods, seeing the logic in my words. Anyone who knows Mr Daniels would know that he wouldn't let something be so out of his control like this. I wish he had been there, had known about this. He would have had a better plan. Maybe Verity would have listened to him and we'd all be free right now.

Hearing Ryan stirring, I turn to him. "Ry?" I ask quietly, hoping he can hear me. Verity knocked him pretty damn hard.

"Why must I have not just one, but two disap-pointments for my children?" Alaric muses aloud to himself. I crawl closer to Ryan and rest my hand on his face as I look at him.

"Ry?" I whisper again.

"Shut up, Kennie. Why so loud?" he grumbles, batting my hand away.

"You can't be serious. Ryan, get the hell up!" I snap, smacking his shoulder lightly, but really, I'm relieved he seems to be okay.

"What are you bitching about?" he questions as

he sits up slowly. His eyes blink open and as he looks between me and Alaric I see the realisation hit him as he remembers exactly what happened before. "Fuck."

"Now you get it," I grumble, before looking up at Alaric "What now, asshole?" I ask.

"Your mother really forgot to teach you two manners," he chastises.

"Shut up!" Ryan snaps, as he stands up on unsteady feet. I follow his movement and we both put our backs to the wall as we face him.

"Oh, she taught us manners. But she didn't teach us to show those manners to psychopathic rebels who want to wipe out the human race," I say. Ryan gives me a look. "What? It's not like he's not already planning to lock us up or kill us for trying to escape? What's the use of us playing nice now?" I ask him.

"That's a fair point," Ryan says, and then he shoves a gust of air at Alaric sending him flying back into the other wall. "Quick!" he shouts, and we sprint for the door. I pull it open, relieved when it clicks and opens with ease, as I'm about to step out, we're both thrown back by a jet of water. I call on my fire mark, and burn through the water creating a wall of steam. I reach for Ry's hand and try to tug him with me back towards the door, but I slide on the wet floor, pulling him to the ground with me. At first I think I've just slipped in the excess water from the jet shot at us, but then I realise exactly what it is. *Verity's blood. Shit.*

"Oh my fucking god," Ryan whispers in a mortified voice, and then I can hear him vomiting behind me. I really hope he didn't get it on my boots. The smoke screen clears, and a few of the rebels walk in and block the door.

Alaric walks over to us, pausing right in front of us, just out of the puddle of blood. "Now, not only are you both disappointments, but you're idiots too. You cannot escape, it is hopeless for you to even try. If you cooperate, we're not intending to harm either of you." He turns his eyes to me. "This is why we had to remove Verity, in order to keep you safe, Mackenzie."

"Safe? Keeping me locked in a compound filled with blood-purity psychos isn't safe!" I growl, feeling a hand rest on my arm.

"Now isn't the right time, Kennie," Ryan warns quietly.

"Perhaps one of you retains some sense at least," Alaric drawls. "Put your hands out," he says. Neither of us move. "Put your fucking hands out now, or I will knock you both out and drag you to your cells by your feet," he says. Begrudgingly we hold our hands out. Iron cuffs are shackled onto our wrists, each with the protection mark engraved into them, as well as the magic itself used to protect others from our marks. *Magic-muting cuffs. Great.*

We're pulled to our feet by a couple of unfamiliar men. Well, they're unfamiliar to me. Ryan is glaring at them in a way that screams he knows them all too well.

"Throw them in separate cells, hell, separate cell blocks for that matter. I don't want any chance of them being able to coordinate another escape attempt. Are we clear?" Alaric demands, and they swiftly nod, tugging us along.

*Great, how are we getting out of here now? And will Enzo and the twins be able to find me in whatever hole he has me thrown into?*

# Chapter 17

LOGAN

"*W*here the fuck is Kenzie?" I ask Daniels, crossing my arms over my chest. Locke is standing firmly at my side, and Enzo on the other.

"She tried to escape with East and Ryan but she failed..." he answers, trailing off as he looks away.

"Well no shit, Sherlock, we know that much already," Enzo snaps, stepping forward towards his friend.

"Verity's dead. They've said Kenzie did it. I've contacted East and he isn't sure what happened with them after he got away. He said Verity was escaping with them and betrayed them, he also said he wasn't sure why Verity was going with them anyway. Apparently Ryan said there wasn't time to explain," he says. His voice cracks a little as he talks about Verity dying, but he covers it quickly, carrying on as if nothing is wrong.

"None of this makes any damn sense," I say, my mind drifts back to my conversation with Kenzie in the shower. She knew we had an escape plan. She knew we'd get her and East out, Ryan too if he wanted to leave. Which we didn't think he did before now. *Something isn't right here... why would she do this and risk everything we had planned?*

"So East has no idea why they were breaking him out that night? Or why Verity was going with him? I don't get why Kenzie wouldn't just wait for us," Locke questions, as if reading my mind. I'd spilled the beans to the others about telling Kenzie the truth. They weren't happy, but I think they were all secretly happy not to have to lie to her anymore. Seeing her hurt like that had been tough for us all.

"He's as confused as the rest of us, but it seemed as if Verity was escaping too, for whatever reason," he answers.

"So they could be lying about Kenzie killing Verity?" Enzo questions.

"Yes, they could," Daniels answers him, but he doesn't sound convinced.

"Kenzie wouldn't have killed her unless she had to, you know that, right?" I say, stepping forward and resting a hand on his shoulder, but he shrugs me off as he steps back away from us.

"She made her views on Verity clear to me before. Verity was past saving. I know she was probably right, but she was my sister, and now she's gone for good. I'll never get a chance to save her now," he replies.

I share a look with Locke. I know I'd never stop trying to save my twin, and he'd be the same with me. Luckily we agreed on most things, like which side of a freaking war to be on. Daniels begins pacing back and forth across the other side of the room

"I'm sorry about your sister, but we need to come up with a plan b," Enzo says, but his voice doesn't sound sorry.

"Could you manage a little more tact?" I whisper, elbowing him in the gut. He rolls his dark eyes at me and then I step in front of Daniels to stop his pacing. It's annoying as fuck, and it's only stressing the rest of us out more.

"Something isn't right about all this, and only you will be allowed to visit Kenz," I tell him and he shakes his head. We need him to see her, find out what happened.

"I need to bury my sister, that's all I need to do," he says and walks out the room before any of us can stop him.

"They aren't going to let us near her, and we need a new escape plan. Daniels is too focused on his sister. We need to plan this on our own," I say, annoyed that Daniels isn't even going to give Kenzie a chance to explain. His emotions are clouding his judgement and I'm hoping he will snap out of it soon.

"What the hell happened last night?" Kelly says as she slams the door open to my room, and quickly shuts it behind her.

"So, Ryan and Kenzie didn't tell you of their escape plan either?" I ask her, and she pulls her white lab coat off.

"No, they damn well didn't. I swear I'm going to kick both their asses when I can see them, but no one will let me in," she says.

Enzo stands up, crossing his arms as he starts to pace. "Kelly, you need to contact your mother, get a plan ready for two days' time. I will get Mr Daniels to go and see Kenzie," he says, before walking around Kelly and out the room.

"How does he plan to do that?" I ask Locke, who shrugs.

"He knew Daniels before the academy," he says, and I look over to see Kelly biting her nails as she looks around.

"Kelly, you okay?" I ask.

"I've barely spoken to my mother in five years, and now I have to ask for her help," she answers in a quiet voice.

"For Kenzie and Ryan, you need to do this," I say gently and she nods, turning around and walking out the room without another word.

"What are we going to do now?" Locke asks, looking as stressed as I feel.

"Train and get stronger, it's all we can do," I say, leaning against the wall and praying that Enzo can convince Daniels to get his shit together.

# Chapter 18

MR DANIELS

"Why are you here? You never liked my sister," I snap at Enzo, hearing him step next to me as I look at the white-painted, wooden box in the ground. I won't admit that some small part of me is happy that someone other than me is also at her funeral, no one should be buried alone. I wish she was alive, so I could shout at her and demand to know what happened. I don't want to believe Mackenzie killed her, she wouldn't do that to me.

"That's not true, I liked her when I was a kid. She brought chocolate cupcakes over to my house," Enzo says quietly, reminding me how he must have met her a few times when we were growing up. He was always following me around, a scared little boy with bruises on his arms, and parents that weren't worth the time of day. I remember the day I walked out from my house, seeing him sitting on the steps, dripping with anger in his dark eyes, but silent. I invited him to my local self-defence class, and then helped him train, helped him learn how to fight back. It wasn't long until I had to go the academy and soon after, my parents were killed. Then Enzo came to the academy and proved to everyone that it doesn't matter what your parents are, you choose your own fate. No one thought that the child of two drunks, with hardly any marks between them, would have eleven marks and be one of the most powerful marked in years.

"I didn't know she did that," I say quietly. Enzo doesn't say anything as I step closer, kneeling down and grabbing a handful of dirt. *Why couldn't Verity be more like Enzo? Why did she have to be like she fucking was?*

"I failed you, Verity. I failed you because as your older brother, I should have protected you. I didn't know about our dad, not until it was too late and the damage he did to you was done. I wish I knew, I wish I hadn't gone to marked academy and left you at home. Maybe if I didn't leave you, you wouldn't have been recruited, then our other parents wouldn't have died saving you," I say, dropping the dirt into the hole. Using my air mark, I swirl the dirt around above the coffin aimlessly.

"You never failed her, you know that right?" Enzo comments, sitting next to me and looking down at her coffin.

"I did. She was so sweet when she was little. How did I not realise what had been done to her?"

"She was, but she changed after she got the pain mark, even at that young age. You just didn't see it, but I did," he explains.

"What?" I ask, dropping the dirt on the coffin and looking at Enzo, wondering what the hell he is going on about.

"I worshipped you growing up, but you know that, and so did Verity. She used to use her pain mark on me, telling me that I couldn't say anything as no one would believe me," he says, making me freeze as I just stare at him. He wouldn't lie to me, I know Enzo well enough to know he wouldn't. My sister did that, my sister who most likely pretended to be sweet and innocent in front of me, and she was doing this the whole time.

"I—"

"Don't say a word to anyone about it or even mention it again. As your friend, I'm just telling you what actually happened. I was a weak, frightened boy whose parents preferred to drink their problems away rather than look after me. I only had you to look up to, and I did anything Verity wanted so I could follow you around," he admits, and I know it's taking a fucking lot for him to admit this to me.

"I didn't have a fucking clue," I admit in shock.

"You lost your sister then, not now," he says, putting a hand on my shoulder.

"I'm starting to think you're right," I reply with a sigh, looking down at the coffin once more.

"But you still have family, hell I've always wanted you as a brother. It's sods law that we would fall for the same girl," he chuckles, almost making me want to smile.

"Mackenzie is hard not to fall for, she's a whirl-wind, that girl," I say, almost smiling until I remember what Alaric said to me.

"She killed Verity," I whisper.

"You don't know that, you've only heard it from Alaric, and no one should trust a word he says," he tells me firmly, and stands up, looking down at the coffin which I can't seem to look away from.

"It's time to say goodbye and then time for you to go and get the answers from our girl," Enzo says, holding a hand out for me. I grab his hand to stand up, and then quickly let go.

"Goodbye, Verity," is all I can say, before calling my air mark and pushing dirt into the hole and watching it fall on Verity's coffin with Enzo's help.

"Are you going to see Kenzie? You're the only one that can," Enzo says once the hole is filled.

"I couldn't stay away, even if I wanted to," I tell him.

"That's Mackenzie for you, I've been the same since I met her," he says, chuckling and walking away. I pull out a small white daisy from my pocket, leaning down and putting it on top of the dirt. I call my earth mark, making the daisy grow into dozens and cover the whole grave. Even if her heart wasn't beautiful before she died, hopefully she can have some peace now. *Or that's what I have to make myself believe to walk away.*

# Chapter 19

MACKENZIE

*I* push around the carrots, peas, and the strange meat that's on the food tray they slid under the door today. It looks like shit and I'd have to be desperate to eat it. I pick it up and slide it back under the door, before going back to my daily pacing. It's been three days since they threw me into this room, the same one East was kept in. The sheets even still smell like him, and I know Alaric put me in here on purpose, as a reminder he had East locked up or maybe a reminder that he is hunting East. It doesn't matter, because I have to believe he's safe.

Jumping when I hear the sound of a key turning, I force myself to stand still as the door opens. Mr Daniels walks in slowly as I let my eyes trail over him. His clothes are wrinkled, his hair is messy and his eyes look tired, he looks nothing like he usually does, but exactly how I expected him to be. He lost his sister, and my heart hurts for him. I wish I could have been there when he found out. I wish I could change everything about that day so that his sister didn't die the way she did.

"Shut the door and don't disturb us," Daniels tells the guard behind him, who nods and closes the door, as I keep my eyes focused on Mr Daniels. There's a tense silence between us, neither of us saying a word as we just stare at each other.

"Why?" he finally asks, his voice cracking, and it breaks my heart to hear it. I've never seen Mr Daniels weak, or anything other than strong, and yet right now, it's the only way to describe him.

"Why what?" I ask quietly, but my voice still seems louder than it should in the otherwise silent space.

"Why did you kill her?" he asks me, making me step back in shock, not expecting him to accuse me of that.

"You think I killed her?" I ask quietly, wondering how he could ever think that of me.

"Did you?" he asks. "I know you hated her, I

know she would have gone after you first, but she was my little sister Mackenzie!" he shouts, looking away from me, "Who I just put into the cold ground. She's dead, and—" he stops, his words just cutting off as if he can't bear to say anymore.

"I'm sorry," I mumble as I step closer, but he steps away from me, shaking his head and looking down at the ground.

"I need to know," he asks so quietly, but it's still a demand.

"Look at me," I ask, stepping closer once more. He looks up from the ground, finally meeting my eyes. I almost want to look away when I see the hurt in them, the pain, but I don't. He deserves for me to look at him, to be strong for him when he can't be.

"I didn't kill her, I tried to save her because my father told me he was going to. And he did anyway, despite how much I did try to save her and I hate myself for that," I say, taking a deep breath. "I gave her every chance to escape, but in the end, she chose to side with my father. He killed her right in front of me," I say, and he still doesn't move or make a sound. I watch as a tear drops onto the floor; he wipes his hands over his face. Something clearly snaps, as he walks over to me, picking me up and slamming me into the wall. He holds his body close to mine, as he grabs my chin so I have to look at him.

"Why the fuck didn't you call me? Let me know what was going on? I could have lost you both because you're so stubborn," he nearly shouts, the emotion in his eyes is hard to look away from and he won't let me anyway. He wants me to feel this, his pain, his worry and most of all, his love. Even if he doesn't say the words, because he can't, I can see it. I can feel it. "You're not alone anymore, we are here for you, and you need to be in this with us or we will lose everything. Don't push me out, don't rely on anyone else that doesn't love you, because they will never protect you like I can. You can never trust them like you can trust me. I'm with you one hundred percent, Mackenzie Crowe," he says and then he crushes his lips onto mine. Mr Daniels uses one hand to lift my ass, pulling me against him as his other hand slides into my hair, controlling the kiss. I reach down, pulling his shirt up and he breaks the kiss to let me pull it off him and my eyes widen at his sculpted chest, the little scars that I can see trailed across it, and the v shape that dips into his pants. That's the only pause we have as we kiss again, our lips harshly battling against each other, as all the frustration we have built up pours out. Mr Daniels pulls my shirt off, pushing down my jeans and underwear in one go. He unclips my bra seconds later, breaking away from my lips as he kisses down my neck and towards my breasts. I moan when he teases me, kissing around the nub before sucking it into his mouth and moving to the next one as he puts his knee between my legs, rubbing against me. He doesn't spend long with my breasts as I slide my hand into his trousers and pull him out, feeling how hard he is.

"Mackenzie, tell me to stop and—" he gasps, placing his forehead on my shoulder as I stroke him.

"Don't you dare fucking stop, Daniels," I say, making him chuckle as he carries me over to the bed. He undoes his trousers, climbing over me and I pull him closer as I kiss him. He slides into me in one harsh, long, and amazing stroke, making my back arch in pleasure.

"You're mine now, Mackenzie," he whispers in an almost growl against my lips, as he keeps thrusting in and out of me. His hand slides down my stomach towards my core, rubbing my clit in perfect circles—driving me insane with the pleasure.

"Daniels," I moan as he bites down on my neck,

and sucking on a spot that I love. I lose control as he makes me come. He quickly follows me, slamming into me so hard that the bed slams against the wall with every thrust, before I feel him finish inside me, and he presses his lips agianst mine as he groans my name.

"This is us now, together. All of us, no more secrets," he says a little breathless.

"All of us?" I ask, needing him to understand.

"I know you love them, and I like them...okay some of them in smaller doses than others, but I like that they love you. They will protect you when I can't," he says, sliding out of me, but keeping his body on top of mine as I trace the pain mark on his ribs.

"You never told me your first name, it feels weird to even ask now," I say, making him laugh. He goes to answer me just as the door is opened. I quickly grab the blanket, covering myself, when I see Logan walk into the room, holding keys and smoke trailing in after him. His eyes widen as he looks between us, before grinning and leaning against the wall.

"Time to leave, naughty student-teacher time will have to continue later," he says, making me laugh a little, while Mr Daniels glares at him as he pulls his trousers up.

"One, not a real teacher. Two, what the fuck are you talking about?" he asks, getting off the bed.

"The council is attacking the base, and Kenzie's father is distracted. It's time to leave," he explains and then a loud alarm rings throughout the place.

"What the hell is that?"

"Oh, I blew up the science labs," Locke answers as he comes into the room and stares at me, and then Mr Daniels for a second before grinning.

"Sexy teacher time?" Locke comments.

"That's what I said," Logan says and then high fives Locke.

"Small doses, *very small fucking doses*," Mr Daniels mutters, making me laugh as I slide out from the bed and quickly grab my clothes.

# Chapter 20

MACKENZIE

he alarms are still blaring as we run across the compound, rushing to the outer wall. We figure with all the guards fighting and distracted, it should be easy enough for us to escape over the edge of the wall. Once outside of the building I was locked in, it is utter chaos. I can't tell who is on whose side, with all the unfamiliar faces and everything moving so fast, so I just try to dodge and stay out of the way of all the fighting marked. Finally, I see three familiar faces, Enzo and Kelly are practically carrying Ryan as they make their way towards us. I stop running, the twins and Mr Daniels notice instantly that I've stopped, and come to a halt too.

"Kenzie, this isn't the time to pause and stretch," Locke shouts.

"We have to wait for the others!" I shout back, pointing at Enzo, Kelly, and Ryan. His eyes lock on them and he jogs towards them, nudging Kelly out of the way to help Enzo and speed them up. Kelly reaches for me as soon as she's close enough, giving me a tight hug.

"Are you okay?" she whispers, and I snort. "Yeah, stupid question," she mumbles sheepishly as she pulls back. She casts a worried glance at Ryan, before moving forward and tugging my hand to pull me along too, not giving me a chance to check on my brother myself. I caught a glance though, and that was enough to see the blood and bruises covering him. *No wonder they're practically carrying him.*

We finally reach the edge of the compound, and I'm about to use my air mark to float up, when a firm hand grips my arm.

"What?" I ask, turning to face Enzo, who's left my brother's side to reach me.

"Look closely," he says, pointing up at the top of the wall. I focus and see the familiar glimmer of a protection shield being held over the edges of the compound.

"We can take it, there's enough of us," I say, about to call on my air mark to float up to it, but he shakes his head.

"We have no idea how many people are holding that up. It may take us too long to bring it down, maybe we won't be able to even bring it down at all. We need to find another way," he says. I cast a worried glance at my brother, who seems barely conscious. *We need to get out of here now, but how….? It's chaos, there's no way we are getting—the tunnels.* The answer hits me like a ton of bricks. Ryan's plan for Verity and East's escape. Verity didn't know about us using the tunnels, so I doubt that they figured out our plan to use them either.

"Come on, I know a way out!" I shout at them, as I take off running towards the direction of the entrance to the tunnels. They trail closely behind me, not even questioning how I know a way out.

We reach the building next to the wall that the entrance is meant to be tucked behind. Just as I'm about to lead them around, a fire ball flies right by my head. I turn around finding a group of rebels standing around us and slowly getting closer. The twins put Ryan down, resting him against the building as they get ready to fight.

"Kenzie, leave!" Enzo shouts as he runs forward to join the twins. I'm not leaving any of them behind, I go to follow him when hands grab my waist and pick me up with ease. He turns with me in his grip and sets me down facing the direction I was previously headed in. I turn around and glare at Mr Daniels.

"I'm not leaving them," I say, already trying to edge past him.

"Don't be stupid. Either you leave now, or I will throw you over my fucking shoulder and make you. Go, I will make sure the others follow." I bite my lip, looking between him and the others. "Go! It's you they need, it's you we need to get away from them, so listen for once in your life and fucking go!" he snaps. I look into his green eyes, feeling hurt at how he spoke to me, but I can see the determination in them. The determination is to keep me safe, and I can't be mad at him for that. I sigh and nod, turning and heading for the tunnel entrance.

I reach the metal cellar doors that lean against the back of the building. I try to pull them open, but they're locked. *Shit.* I can hear so much shouting from around the building as I call on my fire mark, melting the lock. As I pull open the metal doors, I pause, debating whether to go or not, but I know that if I don't, all of this has been for nothing.

I walk down the steep, stone steps, and call on my fire mark again, picturing a fireball hovering harmlessly in the air to light the dark space. The fireball appears and I look around, looking for the trap door Ryan told me about, the one that leads to the tunnels. The musty smell of the cellar makes me want to sneeze as I look for something that stands out on the floor. Spotting a brown rug on the far side of the room, I sprint across and pull the dusty rug out of the way. Clearly this wasn't a way used often, considering all the dust. Sure enough, under the rug is the trap door. Pulling it open, this time I don't hesitate, gripping onto the cold metal bars as I make my way down. I call my fireball to follow me, as I don't like the idea of heading down here in the dark alone.

I hear footsteps above me, people are coming into the basement. I go to step down onto the next bar, but my foot hits the ground instead. I step back and look up, watching to see if it's friend or foe that has followed me. I breathe a sigh of relief when I see Locke's face grinning down at me. I lean back against the wall waiting for him to climb down. As soon as he reaches the ground he pulls me to him, pressing his lips to mine. I kiss him back, but it's over all too quickly as he pulls away.

"I'm so glad you're okay," he says, and then Logan drops down next. He's quickly followed by Enzo, and then I stare up, looking for the others, but there's no sign of Kelly, Ryan, or Mr Daniels.

"Come on, which way is it?" Logan asks, sliding his hand into mine.

"South, but where are the—"

"There's no time, come on. Ryan said we had to make you leave," Enzo says, heading left. Logan follows him, pulling me along after him. Locke brings up the rear, keeping close to me.

We run at first, but to a fast walk after a while. We must nearly be at the exit when I hear another set of footsteps following us. I wait until we turn the next corner before slowing.

"Guys," I whisper, tugging Logan's hand to get his attention. He comes to a halt, and so do I. Locke stumbles right into me.

"Why are we stopping?" he groans, clearly unhappy.

"What are you idiots doing?" Enzo says, walking back to us. I pull a face at how loudly he is speaking, hoping that whoever is behind us didn't

162

hear him. He'd been ahead of us the whole time, but he never let us fall too far behind.

"Listen," I say quietly, and they all seem to tense up as they hear the footsteps. Only one set.

Locke moves to stand in front of me, and Enzo moves closer as we wait for whoever it is to turn the corner. I can feel the tension coming from all of them, and silently pray it's the others coming, and not rebels. The twins' shoulders relax, and they step out of the way so I can see who it is.

"You made it," I say, stepping past the twins to fall into Mr Daniels' arms. He presses a kiss to my forehead, and I step back and peer around him, looking for sign of Ryan and Kelly. "Where are they?" I ask him, feeling worried.

"They... I couldn't get back to Ryan. They'd pushed me and Kelly right back. She wouldn't leave without him. She told me to go, to make sure you got out," Mr Daniels says.

"You left my brother and my best friend there?" I ask incredulously, as I try to step past him. I need to go back.

"Don't be stupid, we've had this conversation. We need to get you out of here," he replies, grabbing my shoulders and not letting me get past. I try and wriggle out of his grip, but it's no use. The others all close in too, none of them are chancing me making a break for it to go back.

"Please, guys," I plead, but they all stand firm.

"Come on, we need to keep moving," Enzo says in a cold voice. The twins at least have the decency to look guilty about leaving Kelly and Ryan, but even they don't say anything as I'm practically herded the rest of the way through the tunnels.

# Chapter 21

MACKENZIE

***S***taring out the car window, I shrug off Locke's arm when he tries to throw it over my shoulders for the second time. He sighs and moves over to the other side of the backseat. Daniels is driving and Logan called shotgun, and I've been sitting back here ignoring all of them since we left, after meeting one of Mr Daniels' council contacts.

They hooked us up with this car, and now we're driving back up to mainland Scotland. From there we will need to get on the ferry to the island, and then we're returning to the academy. I said I wanted to go home, but my idea was quickly vetoed. Apparently, the school has better security than my home. They also conveniently ignored me when I pointed out the fact the security wasn't so stellar at the academy, considering that I had been taken from there last time.

Enzo had gone with his sister, Stacey, who as well as being the spirit teacher at the academy, is also apparently contracted by the council for something. He didn't explain what she was doing there, just that he would meet us at the ferry and then drive up to the school with us.

"Kenzie, you can't ignore us all the entire way back," Locke says quietly. I notice that Logan turned up the music now blaring from the car stereo, just a second before Locke spoke. I turn and glare at the back of Logan's head. They must have twin telepathy or something, that was way too convenient for them. I don't answer Locke, as that would defeat the purpose of the silent treatment, if I broke it to tell him that he was getting the silent treatment. They all are.

"Kenzie, please don't be like this," he pleads in a low voice. I try to take a look at him in the car's rear-view mirror, but it's not angled right for me to be able to catch him in the reflection from back here. I try to sneak a glance at him, but he's staring at me. I'm not able to look away, caught in his eyes' intense gaze like a deer trapped in headlights.

"Talk to me," he whispers, breaking me from my trance.

"You all just left them," I blurt out, and a hurt look crosses his face. He swallows thickly, his eyes darting away from mine as if he can't look into them.

"We didn't just leave them, we had no choice. Getting you out and safe was the priority, both Kelly and Ryan knew that. They'll be happy you're safe, and you know we will rescue them as soon as we can," he answers.

"But what if that isn't soon enough, what if he hurts them?" I snap, feeling my fingernails digging into my palms. I relax my hands and look down, spotting the little crescent-shaped indents from my nails, a couple of them even broke the skin. I wipe my hands off on my jeans, the tiny bit of blood not even leaving a mark on them. Locke grabs my hands and pulls them to his lips; he kisses one and then the other gently.

"He won't kill either of them, I won't lie and say they won't be harmed, but they won't be killed, and we will get them back. We will get them as soon as we can. We care about them too, Ryan is our friend."

"But he's my brother, and Kelly is my best

friend. We spent so much time together growing up. She basically lived at our house, because her parents were always too busy for her. She'd sometimes sleep over for weeks at a time, and her parents wouldn't even notice," I explain quietly. When he doesn't say anything back, I continue. "She spent most holidays with us, nearly every Christmas and New Years since we became friends. Whenever we went abroad, her and East would come with us. East would obviously be there with Ryan, but me and Kelly would follow them around. Ryan hated it back then, I'm not sure when he started liking Kelly, he never seemed to like her when we were younger. She was like a bonus annoying sister back then," I ramble on, I barely notice as he scoots closer. This time I don't stop him as he wraps his arm around me.

"What was the last holiday you went on?" he asks.

"We went skiing in France," I say, pulling a face at the memory. "I hate the cold, and I was so terrible at skiing. East was naturally amazing at it, I swear he's always annoyingly good at things. Ryan could keep up, and Kelly could ski just fine, but instead she chose to keep me company. On the last day of the trip, we basically raided the booze, and got drunk in the lodge while my mum and dads went skiing with East and Ry. We ended up drinking so much, and then we fell asleep before we could clean up."

"I can guess your parents weren't thrilled when they got back?" he asks in a humorous tone. I smile wryly.

"Instead of telling us off, they quietly opened the door again, and then they used the air mark to move some of the snow from outside into the cabin, and they dumped it all over the two of us. We were completely covered and still slightly drunk when we were shocked awake like that. I was shivering for ages after, and I was so mortified at East laughing at me," I say, fully grinning now as I picture it.

"I bet," he replies, smiling too.

"I'm sorry for being moody with you guys, I know it's not your fault. You wouldn't have left them if there was another way," I mumble.

"You don't have to say you're sorry; I know you're just worried about them, all of us are. We will get them back, but first, we need to get you back to the academy and keep you safe. You can't go anywhere without one of us from now on, Kenzie. We can't trust anyone else with you, not when the rebels could be recruiting anyone."

Locke's arm tightens around me, hugging me close to his side. I rest my head against him.

"That's okay with me, I don't want to be away from any of you anyway," I admit.

"You won't. Don't worry, we're all going to stick to you like glue," Logan's voice says from the front. He reaches a hand out behind him and I take it in mine, feeling him squeeze mine comfortingly. After a moment, I notice the car is noticeably silent.

"When did you turn the music off?" I ask, not having noticed.

"When you started talking about Kelly staying with you," Mr Daniels answers plainly.

"Oh," I breathe.

"Mrs Curwood seems to be a very unfeeling woman. I was shocked when she was so unconcerned at Kelly taking part in the mission, but it's becoming less shocking, and more disheartening the more I hear about her," he admits.

"None of the Curwoods are very feeling-focused," I reply.

"Other than Kelly," Logan says.

"Other than Kelly," I echo in agreement. Kelly is one of the most empathic people I have ever met. I never understood how she came out the way she did, when her parents were as cold as they were to her growing up.

I picture her in my head, wishing more than ever she was here with us, returning to the academy. It's hard enough to worry about my brother, without having to worry about the friend I think of as a sister too.

"She'll be okay. Both of them will," Locke says reassuringly. I snuggle into his chest and don't reply, trying to push the worried thoughts from my mind and rest a little for the remainder of the journey.

# Chapter 22

MACKENZIE

"It feels like I haven't seen this place in forever. The last time I was here I had Kelly at my side," I say quietly as we drive up to the academy. The old building looks like it could fall right off the cliff, and yet, it looks nothing like that inside. The typical Scottish cold and wet weather makes everything seem darker, even if it's the middle of the day.

"She speaks, I wondered how long it would take. You haven't said a word to me since I met you at the ferry," Enzo says dryly. I kick the back of his seat, enjoying the shocked glare he turns to give me.

"My brother and best friend are still with that psychopath!" I shout at him, my earlier anger flaring again, but Locke puts his hand on my shoulder, grounding me.

"They are our friends as well, and we will get them back," Locke reminds me.

"Enzo, was Ryan in that state when you got him out?" I ask.

"Do you really want the answer to that, Crowe?" he says, almost gently this time, his dry tone from before gone. It's nothing like I'm used to hearing him speak to me.

"No, I don't, but I need to know," I reply.

"Yes, he was," he says, and I look away, as Mr Daniels parks the car in front of the academy. I wait for Locke to get out, before sliding out myself, and walking straight up the old steps to the cave entrance.

"Miss Crowe, it is a pleasure to see you again, and looking well," Mr Lockhart says as he walks out the cave, making me stop in my tracks. I feel the twins stand next to me, and I watch as Mr Lockhart looks over at Mr Daniels.

"Mr Daniels, is everyone okay? Do the healers need to be called?" he asks, looking at our ripped and dust-covered clothes. Mr Daniels has blood on his shirt, not his own, but Mr Lockhart wouldn't know that.

"Not needed, but a meeting is," he says, walking over to Mr Lockhart, who looks back at me.

"I will call Miss Curwood and some of the teachers. They are all that are here as the rest are part of the current attack."

"Have they taken the base?"

"Yes, but it seems that there were escape vehicles we were not aware of, and many escaped, including Alaric, his son and Kelly Curwood," Mr Lockhart says, and Locke wraps an arm around me as I try to think of something, anything else. *We don't know where they are, so how the fuck can I help them now?*

"Come in, come in. You must all be tired and need some rest,"

"I don't need to rest, what I need is to get to this meeting to plan a way to save my brother and best friend," I say, stepping out of Locke's embrace, and walking up the steps to Mr Lockhart.

"I don't believe that's the best idea, Miss Crowe," he disagrees.

"Let her, this is about her and her family after all," Mr Daniels suggests, stepping closer and reaching down to link our hands together.

"Personal relationships between students and

174

teachers are not allowed," Mr Lockhart says, shaking his head.

"I'm no teacher and I've never really been one, now let's sort this meeting out," he says, turning and pulling me with him into the caves.

"Kenzie?" I hear my name whispered around the corner of the cave, just before East appears. He runs to me as I let go of Mr Daniels.

"East," I shout in relief, throwing my arms around his neck as he holds me close.

"Fuck, I've been so worried," he says, pulling back so he can kiss me.

"I'm back," I whisper against his lips and he grips me to his chest again. I turn my head to the side, opening my eyes to see Mr Daniels standing in the shadows, watching us. He smiles, before walking down deeper into the caves.

---

"WHAT THE HELL is *she* doing here?" I say, glaring across the room at Stella who leans against the wall, watching me with a big smirk on her lipstick covered lips. We just left East, Enzo, and the twins in the cafeteria to come here for the emergency meeting they called. I look around the room, seeing most of the teachers I had, even if my classes feel like years ago already.

"Stella's parents are undercover with the rebels, they're guards. She might have information for us," Mr Daniels tells me. I try not to look at her as I take a seat on the massive table, and Mr Daniels sits down next to me.

"It is good to have you back at Marked Academy, Miss Crowe," Miss Tinder says, sitting opposite me and I can feel that not a word she just said was true.

"Your hair is growing back nicely I see," I say with a smile, and she smacks her hand on the table, her eyes burning with hate.

"Enough childish conversations, I want to hear what happened last night and why we are missing two of our people," Mrs Curwood says as she comes into the room, sitting at the top of the table next to Mr Lockhart. It hurts to see her, as she looks so much like Kelly. They have the same curly blonde hair, blue eyes, and even similarities with their faces. Mrs Curwood is nothing like her daughter; she is as heartless as they get.

"Two people? One of those people is your daughter," I say, and she waves a hand at me dismissively.

"I wasn't asking you," she replies emotionlessly, "Mr Daniels, please tell me the events that happened and how you escaped." I hold in the urge to snap at her as Mr Daniels puts his hand on my knee, rubbing circles in comfort.

"We escaped using the tunnels. I couldn't get Kelly or Ryan away as we were separated, and they were too far from the entrance."

"Fine, but I want a detailed report of every event in the compound, and your escape," she says, lifting two pieces of paper off the table.

"We have no information of the whereabouts of the rebels at this time, but we expect to have some soon, thanks to Stella's parents," she says, putting the papers down and I stand up, watching them all turn towards me.

"They won't give up until they find me, because they want the twelfth power. Now, don't you all think it's time I know what it is?" I say and they all look at each other, equal looks of nervousness and panic.

"I will tell you, but not here," Mr Daniels says, standing up, and taking my hand as several teachers gasp.

"Excuse us for the night, it has been a long day as I'm sure you all know. We will discuss our options in the morning after Stella has had time to contact her parents," Mr Daniels says, not waiting for a response as he puts his arm around my waist, and leads me out the room.

"You know what the twelfth power is and you never told me?" I ask, feeling a little hurt.

"I couldn't while we were there, not when there was a chance someone could hear and let Alaric know I told you," he replies.

"I get it, I just feel like my life is full of more secrets and pain than anything else," I reply. He pulls me closer as we walk outside the academy, and through the woods.

"It's not always going to be like this, I will make sure of it," he whispers to me, a promise if I've ever heard one.

"Your cabin?" I ask.

"I asked the others to come, and stay here tonight. It's safer than in the main buildings and we have room, but you're in my bed," he whispers the end part in my ear.

"Okay," I chuckle. We walk up to his cabin, where the lights are already on, and he lets me go to open the door.

"Hey, how did it go?" Locke says, stepping out

the kitchen with only some shorts on and a bag of crisps in his hand.

"Good," I reply, seeing East and Enzo step out of one of the bedrooms, with Logan following them.

"Time for some answers, why don't you start?" I ask, turning to Mr Daniels and he nods. I walk past them all and take a seat on one of the chairs, crossing my legs as they all stare at me, and then look back at Mr Daniels.

"The twelfth power is said to be the power to open a portal between Earth and Ariziadia," Mr Daniels says, and none of us can utter a single word as he explains. "The council knows what the power can do, well those at the top do anyway. They keep it from everyone, both due to the fact it's so rare for anyone to be marked with the twelfth mark, and that the mark can cause devastation. You're essentially splitting the barrier between the worlds, and that can go wrong, causing damage to both worlds."

After letting the fact that I can open a portal between worlds set in, I feel like I have a million questions, and no idea which to begin with. Mr Daniels takes a seat on one of the sofas.

"Are you okay, Kenz?" East asks softly.

"I'm...fuck, I have so many questions." I turn

back to face Mr Daniels. "Why wouldn't the council use people with the twelfth mark to go to Ariziadia? Why would they act like it isn't even a real place if they know there's a freaking power to get there? Is that how the marked came to earth in the first place?" The questions all seem to tumble out of my mouth in a string of word-vomit.

"Firstly, because of the risks involved, both for the marked, and for those around them. Secondly, it's much easier for people to accept it's a story. It being real generates a lot of questions that they don't have the answers too. And finally, we believe so." He pauses as everyone else sits down too. "There's an ancient text they keep hidden in a vault underneath the main council building in London. I've never seen it myself, I don't have the clearance for that, but I've heard there's a lot in there, more than they'd ever admit to having information on. One of the sections in the text includes the telling of the crossing, they spent many years working on the translation. It doesn't state how they did it, just how they prepared, and how they found the world here, but the twelfth mark is shown at the top of the page," he explains. As he finishes, I let out a deep breath. *Damn.*

"That's a lot of information to process," I say.

"Do you have any more questions?" he asks.

"Tons," I admit, and then I can't hold in the yawn that escapes.

"It can wait, she needs sleep," Enzo says protectively.

"But I need to know--"

"You can know tomorrow. You need rest," Locke says, agreeing with Enzo as he cuts me off. I hear a phone buzzing and I look around as Mr Daniels pulls his phone out of his jean pocket.

"I have to go back up to the school. Will you five be okay without me?" he asks, and we all nod. He doesn't look happy to be leaving at all. He stands, walking over to the door, I follow after him.

"Going somewhere, Kenz?" East asks with a knowing smirk.

"I'm just saying goodbye, I'll be back inside in a second," I answer, following him out the door. I shut it behind us for a little privacy. "What do they need you for?"

"Nothing they couldn't have done themselves, I'm sure," he answers dryly, grabbing me by the waist, and pulling me to him. I tilt my head up as he leans down to kiss me. His hands grip my hips tightly as we kiss. His phone starts vibrating again, interrupting us, and I groan.

"Can't they wait five minutes?" I mutter.

"If I stay any longer, I definitely wouldn't be leaving in five minutes," he replies, making me laugh lightly.

"Go on then, I'll see you later," I say, and then give him another quick kiss.

"I'll hurry back," he replies, he walks backwards as he steps away, his green eyes watching me intently, before finally turning away as I open the door again.

## Chapter 23

MACKENZIE

*S*tepping into Mr Daniels' bedroom, I'm surprised to find Logan and Locke both stretched out across the bed. "Does Daniels know you two are in here?" I ask, and they both grin mischievously.

"Well, it's so cold in this cabin, we figured we would keep you warm," Logan says.

"Poor East is stuck spooning with Enzo in your room," Locke adds humorously, as he stands up, and crosses the room to me.

"I suppose I could use the extra warmth." Locke smiles at my words, and then leans down to kiss me. His hands slide into my hair while I feel another pair of hands slide around my waist as

Logan's warm body presses against mine from behind.

Logan leans in even closer, pressing kisses to my neck and down to the top of my shoulder. I slide my hands under Locke's shirt, feeling across his hard abs and trying not to moan at how amazing he feels. I pull one of my hands back, reaching behind me to do the same to Logan, but I notice he's already pulled his shirt off. *Sneaky.* I run my fingers along the top of the waistband of Logan's jeans teasingly, letting my fingers slide just beneath it. In response to my teasing, he bites down on my neck playfully, before kissing away the sting.

Locke grabs my waist, turning me around to face his brother. I look at Logan, wanting to just melt into him, he looks so good with his shirt off. I wrap my hands around his neck and pull him down to kiss him. He bites my lip, making me gasp against him, and he darts his tongue in to mingle with mine. I hear the distinctive sound of a zip being undone behind me. Locke's hands pull my top up from behind, and Logan pulls back for a moment, breaking our kiss so Locke can get it off.

He leans down to kiss me again, and as he does, I reach for the buttons on his jeans. I slowly unbutton them, my fingers trembling slightly from a mixture of nerves and excitement. He pulls back looking down at me as I lick my lips. I slowly tug his jeans down, and he steps out of them as they hit the floor, leaving him in only his boxers. I turn my head, seeing that Locke is standing in just his boxers too. I unbutton my own jeans, sliding them off easily. I climb onto the bed, feeling a little nervous as I look between them both. I've never slept with two guys at once before. I knew there was always a good possibility it would happen at some point, but I'd never really let myself be convinced of it before now.

"Are you okay with this?" Locke asks, as he slides onto the bed next to me.

"Yeah, we can wait if you're not," Logan adds, crawling onto the bed on the other side of me.

"I want this. I want both of you," I answer. I reach a hand up behind me and unclip my bra, letting it fall. They both watch, staring at me intently like there is no one else in the world. I'm not sure who to touch first, what to do but I know I'm going to enjoy figuring it out. Locke's hands reach out for me, so I slink closer to him. He trails his hands from my hair, down my neck, then to my shoulders as he teases me. His hands then move around, brushing across my chest, teasing as they slowly move across my nipples. Hands rest on my hips from behind as Logan peppers kisses across the back of my neck and shoulders. I slide on top of Locke, kissing him fiercely as Logan moves up the bed towards the headboard.

Feeling Locke's hardness pressing up against me, I slide down onto him fully, moaning as I do. Logan moves closer to me, and I reach for his cock, stroking it in my hand a few times before taking him into my mouth. Locke thrusts up into me, and a breathy moan escapes my lips around Logan. Locke slides his hand down between us, pressing his fingers against me and rubbing in torturous circles as he continues to thrust into me. I suck harder as I feel Locke pick up speed, just as Logan's hands slide into my hair, as he takes control of my mouth. I lose all control when Locke's expert fingers make me come, just as he finishes inside me, gripping my hips tightly. A few more thrusts into my mouth, and Logan comes as I grab his ass, keeping him in place as I swallow. We all collapse back onto the bed, breathless, and Locke pulls a blanket over us.

"We are so lucky to have met you Kenzie," Locke whispers, pulling my body against his as Logan pulls one of my legs over his hip.

"I think I'm the lucky one," I yawn, before slowly drifting off to sleep.

---

"HAVE A GOOD NIGHT?" Enzo asks me, making me jump and drop my coffee, but he catches it with his air mark, floating it back into my waiting hands.

"You scared the shit out of me," I exclaim, leaning back against the counter as I look out the window at the sunrise. It's painting oranges, pinks and red across the sky, it's really pretty to look at.

"You never answered my question, Crowe," Enzo asks, stepping closer to me, and pushing his body into mine as he reaches for the kettle behind me.

"Do I need to? You know I did because you heard," I shrug, and he grins as he gets a cup out of the cupboard and adding coffee to it. He pours his water in and adding a little milk, while I just watch him. His black hair is longer than it has been in a while, dropping into his dark eyes a little but it just adds to how good looking he is. He has on jeans and a tight, white shirt that sticks to his muscular frame, making it a little hard to look away.

"You're right, I did, and you know what?" he

asks me, sipping his coffee before putting it down, not saying a word until he steps in front of me. He takes my coffee from me, putting it on the side and leaning down to whisper in my ear. "I would usually be jealous to hear the girl I'm fucking mad for moaning, and fucking someone else, but it didn't make me *jealous*."

"What did it do?" I ask breathlessly.

"Turned me on so damn much, Crowe," he says, turning to kiss me harshly. He picks me up and slides me onto the counter as my legs go around his waist. We pause when a door is slammed shut. Enzo moves away from me, muttering curses under his breath as we turn to see Mr Daniels. He looks worn out as he leans against the door, his head bowed.

"Long night?" I ask him and I pick up my coffee, pretending like I wasn't seconds away from sleeping with Enzo on the kitchen counter. *Damn, that would have been some good sex.*

"Meetings, and then we just found out Stella's parents are dead," he says. I instantly feel sorry for her; despite how much I hate her, I wish she didn't have to go through that.

"Shit," Enzo mutters loudly. I slide off the counter, walking over to Mr Daniels.

"Then how are we going to find my brother and Kelly?" I ask.

"I don't know, Miss Crowe, I haven't got a clue and I hate it," he answers, sending dread through me as he pulls me to his chest, while I try not to panic.

# Chapter 24

MACKENZIE

---

"*You* should answer the door, I know it's for you," Mr Daniels says as I lift my head off his chest and frown at him in question. I slide off him, walking over to the door, and pulling it open to see my mum standing there, with Dad P right behind her.

"Mum, Dad?" I say, just before my mum pulls me to her and squeezes me tightly.

"Oh, Kennie, I swear I will kill Alaric for what he has done to my children," she whispers, loud enough that Dad P hears and gives me a worried look as he steps closer, and puts his hand on my cheek.

"You have grown up so much, I can tell just by

looking at you," he says, and my mum finally lets me go so Dad P can hug me.

"Hello," I hear Mr Daniels say and I turn to see him in the doorway.

"Would you like to come in, Mr and Mrs Crowe?" he asks, and I quickly wipe my tears away as my dad lets me go.

"Now you must be Mr Daniels, the one that called us and got us transport here in such short notice?" Dad P asks, walking around me and offering Mr Daniels a hand to shake. They introduce themselves and when Mr Daniels looks over at me, I mouth *"Thank you,"* at him.

"Mrs C?" East says behind Mr Daniels, who steps out the way to let my mother go to East. She hugs him tightly, and pulls back.

"Your mother is worried sick about you, now go to your room, and call her right now," she says, and East loses all colour in his cheeks as he nods and walks away.

"Now, what is the plan for saving my son and making sure no one ever touches my daughter again?" my mum asks, her hands resting firmly on her hips.

"We finally have a location," I hear one of my

other dads say in the distance, and I turn to see Dad M and Dad L walking out from the woods. I run to them, hugging them both as they give me relieved looks.

"I want to ask how you are, but it seems like a stupid question," Dad M asks, as I pull away from him.

"Not good, but a location? Do you know where Ry is?" I ask.

"Why don't we take this inside?" Mr Daniels suggests once more and this time we all go in, finding spots on the sofa to sit. East and Enzo come out the room, followed by Locke and Logan who all introduce themselves before finding walls to lean on near the chair I sit in. East sits on the arm of my chair, and Mr Daniels sit on the other one. My mum gives me a knowing look as she looks between all my guys and how close we all are, before winking at me, making me smile for the first time in a while.

"Now Kenzie, I don't want you to freak out when I explain this all to you? Okay?" Dad M asks, as East slides his hand into mine.

"Okay?" I question nervously. Telling someone not to freak out, actually just makes them freak out, so I never got the point of people saying that.

"We received images from a guard undercover with the rebels, who we thought was dead, showing us a rough location in a local shipping yard not far from here," he says, and I smile before feeling confused.

"Wait, why would I freak out about that?" I ask and Dad L takes over.

"They also showed Kelly beaten and tied up."

"No!" I shout, horror filling me as I stand up, and shaking my head in disbelief. *Ryan wouldn't let that happen to Kelly, and if he couldn't stop it, what have they done to him?*

"Show me the photos and then we need to go there right now!" I demand, and my parents all look at me.

"The rescue and attack party leaves tomorrow morning, but you will not be going," mum says gently.

"I can't stay here when she needs me!"

"I will go to get her and Ryan back, with some of the others. Your parents are right, you can't come and get captured. It's what they want," Mr Daniels says, and my guys all mumble agreements.

"I know you're right, I just can't bear the thought of her dying while I stay here and do nothing," I say, feeling useless because I know I can't go.

"We are all going as well, and I will heal her as

soon as I can," Dad P says and my mum gets up, walking over to me.

"I will stay with you in the academy because I'm not a good fighter or healer. I want to go to save Ryan, but I know when it's not the time to be over-protective, and when it's time to trust your partners," my mum tells me before turning back to the rest of the room. "Let's go back to the main school and leave Mackenzie with her boyfriends to discuss this. I could use a drink," she says and my dads all get up, kissing me on the cheek before leaving.

# Chapter 25

MACKENZIE

"hat do you mean, you want me to go to class? You've got to be joking," I say, gaping open-mouthed at the two headmasters standing in the doorway to Mr Daniels' cabin. They'd shown up, asking why I hadn't gone to class, as it had started fifteen minutes earlier, and they were expecting that I would attend. *What the hell are they thinking?*

"We think it would be best to return you to a level of normalcy," one of them says.

"You and Mr Black will remain here, and resume your classes, whilst the others will be assisting Mr Daniels and the council," the other adds.

"You can't just expect me to go back to my

classes, to act like nothing ever happened?" I sputter, not believing they could really suggest something so incredulous.

"That is not what we are suggesting, Miss Crowe. We simply believe that it would be best for you to resume your schedule as soon as possible. You're already behind now as it is," the first replies firmly. He goes to step into the cabin, but I hold firm. I doubt Mr Daniels would want them in here.

"But with everything going on, can't it wait?" I whine pathetically. I really don't want to go. Everyone will be looking at me after what happened.

"No. The decision is final, and you are already late for class. You should get going now, before you miss the whole thing," the other answers.

"Fine, give me five minutes to say goodbye and get changed. What day is it anyway?" I question, and they both give me exasperated looks.

"It's Monday, Miss Crowe," he answers dryly.

*What classes do I even take on Monday?* Headmaster Lockhart must see my confusion, as he lets out a deep sigh.

"You're currently meant to be in healing class, followed by pain this afternoon," he says in an unamused tone.

"Great, thanks," I say, and then I slam the door shut in their faces. I'm too pissed over having to go back to classes already to care about how rude that may have been.

"You didn't just...?" East asks as he walks in from the bathroom.

"Maybe." I shrug. It's too late to worry about that now.

"You're probably going to live to regret doing that," he says in a serious tone, but his eyes are shining with amusement.

"Yeah, yeah. I'll risk it. Where are the others?" I ask. I hadn't seen the others since late last night. It had been eerily quiet in the cabin this morning. I'd fallen asleep on the sofa, and I woke up tucked up in Mr Daniels' bed, alone. I had much preferred the large bed with company.

East hesitates before answering, "They already left to get Ryan and Kelly. They left at about five in the morning, they didn't want to wake you since you've been getting so little sleep."

"We were all still up talking at one, they couldn't have had any sleep," I say, my worried feeling slipping into my tone. East crosses the room to me and pulls me into his arms.

"It'll be fine. They'll be okay. They planned on

sleeping in the car on the way to the meeting point. Someone else is driving, so they'll all have a chance to catch a few hours," he reassures me. I bite my lip, not quite believing that they'll actually sleep. I hate the idea of them going into a fight when they haven't even gotten enough rest. He rests his fingers under my chin and tilts my head up so I'm looking into his hazel eyes. "Don't worry yourself about them, Kenz. They've got this," he says softly, brushing his other hand across my cheek tenderly.

I open my mouth to argue all the reasonable reasons I have to worry, but he silences me by pressing his lips against mine. He kisses me softly, and then pulls away to look at me.

"East, I can't help but—"

He cuts me off, crashing his lips back against mine harder this time. I return his kiss eagerly, as his hands thread roughly into my hair, and he walks me back to the wall. My back slams into the cold wall, feeling the chill set into me quickly. He slides one hand down my body, resting it on my hip, gripping it tightly. His teeth graze my lower lip, and he moves his body closer to mine, trapping me tightly against the wall. I'm not so cold with his hot body against mine. I manage to pull away, just about convincing myself that I do indeed have to go to class. I probably pushed my luck as it is with the door slam.

"Sorry, but we have to go to class," I say. I really don't want to go though. I never wanted to go to this damn school anyway, and I was right not to want to be here, considering all the trouble that's happened. But there have been good things too, I muse as I look at East.

"Class...that's what they wanted? You can't be serious?" he questions, his eyebrows shooting up.

"So serious, and they said you had to go to my classes with me rather than your own." I sigh. "I need to get changed, I slept in these clothes," I say, gesturing down at my crinkled jeans and top. Luckily I'd already tamed my long, black hair back in a thick, high ponytail.

"I should probably change too," he concedes, stepping back. I look at him properly, noticing the tight grey workout top and black joggers he's wearing. The top clings to him, showing off every muscle. *Does he really have to get changed?*

"If you keep looking at me like that, we're not going to class, Kenz," he says in a low tone.

"Is that a threat or a promise?" I ask teasingly, and he steps closer again, leaning down so his lips brush my ear slightly, making me shiver.

"A promise, and I always keep my promises," he answers. He then pulls back again, and heads for my room, where he and the others have stashed their clothes. I watch him as he goes, and then groan to myself. *I'm going to have to follow him in there to get my clothes too, damn it!*

I move slowly across the sitting room, creeping into my room quietly. East has his top off, and is rummaging through a backpack for another. He turns around, catching me staring at him. He grins, crossing the room to me and leans around me to shut the bedroom door.

"What are you doing?" I ask innocently, even as I flutter my lashes a little.

"I don't break my promises, Kenz," he says, he steps closer to me, and I move back.

"We're going to get in trouble," I say slowly, taking another step as he matches mine. He moves in time with me, watching me like a predator eyeing up its dinner. My back hits the wall.

"They'll live," he whispers, and then he pounces. His arms pin me to the wall, and his lips easily find mine again. Slinking my arms around his neck, I jump up, wrapping my legs around his waist tightly, feeling his hardness press against me just right. I moan into his mouth as he grinds his hips against me, and he pushes me even tighter between him and the wall. There's no way we're leaving this room anytime soon now.

We were already late, might as well just try and be on time for the next class instead, this one's a lost cause. I smile as he pulls his lips from mine to kiss along my jaw. So worth missing class for.

# Chapter 26

MACKENZIE

*D*espite the best of intentions, we are still running late as we rush through the main building to pain class. The door of the room is still open, so we can't hover outside when we get there. The teacher, Mr Tower, is leaning against his desk watching the door. He scowls at us both as we walk in slowly, hand in hand.

"Mr Black, I wasn't aware you were joining us today. Did you suddenly develop the pain mark over night?" he asks mockingly.

"No, sir. I'm just sitting in," East replies politely.

"And you, Miss Crowe, after Mr Anders informed me you missed healing class earlier, despite Headmaster Lockhart's reassurances you would be attending, I assumed you must have fallen gravely ill. What other possible excuse could you have?" Mr Tower says, as he slicks his greasy, black hair back. He gives a pointed look between me and East, and I glance away from him to look around the room.

Stella is sitting there with a wide grin on her face. She's dyed the tips of her hair purple since I've last seen her. I normally love seeing colours in people's hair, but on Stella, the purple looks tacky. Especially considering her top is the exact same shade of purple.

"I wasn't feeling great earlier, but I'm feeling much better now," I lie, and then I head towards the only two free seats together, tugging East along after me. Unfortunately for us, that puts us right next to the desk where Stella is sitting alone. Dropping his hand, I quickly snag the seat further away, leaving East to take the spot between me and Stella. Only a small gap to walk between separates them. He gives me a dirty look as I grin evilly at him from my secured spot. Without any other option, East settles down in the seat.

"Now, before we were so rudely interrupted by a late student, where were we?" Mr Tower asks the class, I can't stop my eyes from rolling at that.

"Something funny, Miss Crowe?" he asks, narrowing his eyes on me. *Shit.*

"No, not at all, Mr Tower," I answer blandly.

"Uncle, she was just whispering things to East. I'm sure I saw her dirty hands sliding onto his lap under the table too," Stella whines. *Lying bitch!*

Both of my hands are flat on the table in front of me, but that doesn't stop my face from flushing hot as everyone in the classroom turns around to stare at me.

"Mr Black, if Miss Crowe cannot keep her hands off you, you will need to leave," Mr Tower says sternly.

"But that's bullshit, she didn't touch me!" East shouts angrily, pushing his chair back. I lay my hand on his shoulder and shake my head slightly at him. Losing his temper isn't going to help either of us.

"She's touching him again," Stella gripes incredulously. *Seriously?*

"I'm touching his shoulder, not his freaking dick. I know you sure as hell aren't a prude, so what's your damn issue?" I ask, snapping at her.

"What are you trying to say?" she growls, standing up and folding her arms. I stand too, not wanting her to tower over me.

"You know exactly what I'm saying," I answer, raising an eyebrow at her as her face contorts in anger. East goes to stand too, but I rest a hand on his shoulder. I don't need him to fight this battle for me. Rebels, I may need help with, but bitchy school girls? I'd dealt with enough of them to know how to handle myself.

"I'd like you to clarify it for me, bitch. From where I'm standing, you're the one getting around. Even a teacher from what I hear," she says in a haughty voice. I hear a few sharp intakes of breath. *Shit. I may know he wasn't here as an actual teacher, but I doubt anyone else does.*

"You're only pissed because none of the guys in this school will touch you even with a ten-foot fucking barge pole!" I snap back.

"Oh really? That didn't stop Enzo coming to see me before he left earlier," she taunts. *Fuck off.*

"Yeah right, like he'd go anywhere near you!"

"Ask him yourself. He dropped by my room around five in the morning, he couldn't keep his eyes, or his *hands* off me." She steps closer to me, her eyes flaring with anger as she tosses her hair back over her shoulder.

"You're lying," I insist. She goes to reply, but the

sound of a book smacking a desk makes us both look to the front of the class.

"Mr Black, please leave the classroom at once. And you, be quiet and take your damn seat!" Mr Tower shouts, and Stella gives me a victorious look, but it's short lived. "You too, Stella. I won't be pleased if I am forced to put my own niece in detention."

"You can't be serious," she splutters disbelievingly, as I quietly slide into my seat. East stands up, leaning down to place a kiss on my forehead. "I'll just wait outside, Kenz. Don't worry, I won't leave you," he whispers in my ear, before he walking out the room. I can still see him through the open door, and he gives me a little wave.

"Deadly serious," Mr Tower answers, his pale, almost translucent face seems flushed with either embarrassment or anger. I suppose nobody wants to hear their niece boasting about hooking up with a guy, especially in the class they are trying to teach. Stella sits down, but pulls out her phone, clearly intending to ignore the rest of her uncle's class. He chooses to ignore the fact she's pulled out her phone, and walks to the door, slamming it shut and cutting East from my line of sight. Asshole.

"Now where were we class?" he asks again in a

tired voice. The whole class stares blankly at him, clearly everyone had gotten lost in the drama. Fantastic. They're all still turning to stare at me, and my face just keeps growing hotter. I feel one of my marks on my wrist burning. *Which one is that...?*

Suddenly, flames erupt all over my desk. I lean back, falling back on my chair and knocking my head on the ground. *Fuck.* After hearing so many teachers tell the exact same story of a student leaning back in their chair, then falling and knocking their heads, I was so sure that it was bull-shit. A freaking wide-spread teacher conspiracy. Now here I am, clutching my damn head, the very moron those stories are told about.

"What the bloody hell are you doing?" Mr Tower shouts. Falling? I look up at the spreading flames. Oh right, I accidentally set fire to my desk. Shit. A jet of water covers the desk, splashing and drenching me in the ice-cold liquid. I look down and notice my white top is completely see-through. Just when I thought It couldn't get any worse. I pull myself into a standing position, and a bright flash goes off right in my face. I blink my eyes clear and stare at Stella, she turns her phone around so I can see the screen.

Flushed cheeks, strands of my hair have come

loose from my ponytail and are sticking up all over the place, and my soaked, now see-through shirt does nothing to hide my pink bra as it sticks to my skin. Fantastic. She turns the phone back around to herself. "And send," she says gleefully.

"Send to who?" I ask, wishing I had a jacket to pull on. I'm really giving the whole class a freaking free show right now. I shiver from the chill the water has left me with. Yeah, I really wish I'd grabbed a jacket.

"Everyone," she answers, shrugging. Her phone vibrates, and I expect more gloating from her, but her face turns stricken. "I have to go," she blurts, and then she rushes from the room without another word.

"Stella!" Mr Tower calls after his niece, he follows her out of the room. I trail after them, needing to at least go back to the cabin and change, or I could go and get a new identity to escape the embarrassment of today. I hear a couple sniggers from my classmates as I walk through the room. Oh yeah, new identity sounds *so good* right now.

"Kenz, what are you...?" East asks, trailing off as he looks down at my shirt. "Nice bra," he comments, and I roll my eyes.

"Yeah, you would think so. You're the one who

helped me pick out which one to wear after breaking my other one when you ripped it off me earlier," I tease. I hear a shocked gasp, and turn. Shit the classroom door is still open. I look down pleadingly at the floor. *Anytime you want to open up a hole and suck me down away from this mess, that would be freaking great.* East walks around me and shuts the classroom door. I turn my head left, spotting Mr Tower following Stella around the corner.

"Can't leave you alone for five minutes, can I?" East asks, as he tugs me towards him.

"You can, but please don't," I reply, sighing as I rest my head against his hard chest.

"I won't. Don't listen to anything she said, Kenz. She's a liar," he says, grabbing my hand and rubbing soothing circles over the palm.

"I'm not, that girl is freaking psychotic," I mutter.

"Good, come on, let's get back to the cabin and get you into some dry clothes, or no clothes? I'm sure there are better ways to keep you warm," he whispers huskily in my ear. A smile curves across my lips.

"I love your way of thinking, East," I reply, pulling back and already tugging him down the corridor after me.

"And I love you," he says, pulling me to a stop so he can kiss me. I kiss him back, feeling his soft, but firm lips on mine. I completely melt into him. East is perfect. He's always been perfect.

"I love you too, Easton Black."

# Chapter 27

ENZO

*I* *open my eyes to see the academy on fire, pieces of stone, rocks, broken doors, and everything you could think off flying around the big blue portal in the middle of where the academy used to be. The portal is just off the cliff, and there are students fighting with rebels spread around, just as many of them alive as there is dead on the floor. I watch myself stand up, shaking off the dust and gravel from all over my clothes.*

*"Crowe!" I scream, running straight towards the portal, and I watch as I push the rocks away with my air mark, before jumping off the cliff.*

"EVERYONE KNOWS THE PLAN? We stick together, no one acts like a fucking hero, or tries any stupid shit," Mr Daniels tells us as the van speeds around a corner. I hold onto my seat so I don't fall off as the vision slips away from me. *What the hell was that? And why would I jump off a cliff?* Logan and Locke are sitting next to me, and Mr Daniels is sitting with two other marked opposite from us in the small van. Kenzie's dads and the other council members are driving to the other side of the warehouse, so we are attacking from both sides. Everything has been planned, and nothing could go wrong.

"We know the plan," Locke says firmly, his hands clenched together, but his tone doesn't sound like he's convinced.

"Good. Nothing can go wrong," Mr Daniels replies, frustration written all over his face. We don't get to talk anymore as the van pulls to a stop, and we all stand up. Mr Daniels opens the van door, jumping out, and we all follow closely behind him. We walk down the quiet road, full of parked up lorries and cars, only the sounds of water in the distance to hear. The road comes out to the docks, and straight across the large river is the warehouse that we know they are in. It looks empty, but we know better. We quietly watch as three marked rebels walk past the doors dressed in all black and making them difficult—but not impossible—to see.

"Everyone remember to use your air mark to propel you through the water, we don't need any of our own drowning," Mr Daniels says, and points a look towards the twins who shrug. We all walk to the edge of the river, and I call my air mark, imagining it covering my whole body before diving into the water. I smooth my hands at my sides, pushing my air mark into them and it shoots me across the dark water. I roll onto my back in the water, keeping my eyes open, and watching out for the edge of the dock above the water as I struggle to hold my breath. What feels like a few minutes passes before the dock comes into view above me, and I turn my air mark off. I swim up to the top and take a deep breath, trying to keep quiet.

A few minutes later, Mr Daniels appears next to me, breathing heavily, and then not long after Locke and Logan pop their heads above the water too. No one says a word as we float under the dock, the wood creaking above us as the rebel guards walk past. Mr Daniels moves first, swimming to the edge of the dock, and pulling himself out. I swim after him, pulling myself out just as a wave of water hits me, sending me flying back into the water. I use my water mark to control the water, and my air mark to push me back out, sending me flying into the air. I fly straight back to the dock, where the council and the rebels are already fighting, some with powers and others with old-looking swords. I fly straight towards Locke and Logan, who are using fire and protection to block the water attacks three rebels are throwing at them. I pull a wave of water with me, slamming it into the sides of the rebels and they crash into the floor as I land next to them. I hold my hands over the water, pushing it down onto all three of them as they struggle to get free. *Lucky that they aren't stronger than I am.*

"Freeze them Logan!" I shout as the twins get to me, knowing I will need help to hold all three of them in ice. Logan puts his hand over mine, freezing the water at the same time as I do. We both pull away just as there's a big roar, and we turn to see Locke has shifted into his giant polar bear, and has a rogue guard in his mouth, swinging him around before throwing him into the water screaming.

"Damn I forget how big he gets," I comment, as the polar bear with glowing blue eyes is five times the size of a normal one, and could swallow a human whole.

"Kenzie said my brother is big, but I think——"

"I didn't mean that," I cut him off as I shake my head, and he grins.

"I know, I thought a bit of humour might help the situation," he says as we watch Locke swipe his massive paw, and throw three rebel guards into the water.

"How the hell do you shift into a panther and your twin into a god damn gigantic polar bear?" I ask, but he doesn't get to answer me as I spot Mr Daniels in the crowd.

"This way," I grab Logan's shoulder, pointing at Mr Daniels near the entrance. We run over, hearing Locke following us, his giant paws smacking across the ground. I pick up a rebel with red hair with my air mark, slamming her into the wall and then stop when I see what Mr Daniels has done. He has opened a massive hole in the dock, and made a whirlpool in the hole that he is throwing the rebels in to. I watch in admiration as he combines his air and fire mark into a flamethrower in the shape of a dragon's head, and rounds the rest of the rebels into a circle, before pushing them into the hole right behind them.

"Inside," Mr Daniels says when he is done, and pauses a bit at the sight of the giant polar bear by my side, despite the fact he knows it's Locke.

"Locke, stay out here and don't let anyone in, it's too small for you in there," he tells him, and Locke lowers his head before turning around. We run in, and just stop, staring at the empty warehouse. There are some boxes in the corner and one small chair in the middle of the room. I run over with the others, and I'm the only one that can read out loud what the note on the chair says.

"You lose," I whisper, shaking my head because I can't believe we have been tricked. Kenzie only has East with her. We need to get to her, protect her. *They can't have her.*

"Fuck no," Logan says, stepping back.

"Where are they?" Kenzie's dads say behind us, snapping us all out of it as we see them running to us.

"They must be with Kenzie at the academy, this is a distraction," Mr Daniels growls, sending the chair flying across the room with his air mark. The floor shakes with a loud bang, and I look over at Mr Daniels in horror as the ceiling collapses and the floor falls through, sending us all crashing into the cold water before any of us can call our marks.

## Chapter 28

MACKENZIE

"I always knew you liked Easton Black," my mum chuckles as she eats her bacon sandwich. She pointedly looks over at East as he's walking out, going back to the cabin to get my phone for me. I left it behind this morning after actually putting it on charge for once. I want it close in case any of the guys or one of my dads call to say they have Ryan and Kelly.

I can't stop thinking about how Kelly could still be hurt, or wondering where the hell Ryan is, as I can't believe he would let anyone hurt Kelly. I might have been mad about them being together at the start, but only because they kept it from me. I know they love each other more than anything. Either one of them would be destroyed if the other was hurt, so it doesn't make a bit of sense that Ryan would let it happen.

"Really?" I ask, forcing a smile, and she laughs. She looks happy, despite the fact her eyes show me the world of worry she's trying to hide from me. My mum usually looks so in control, so carefree, but hasn't recently, not that I can blame her. I can't say anything about my mum's messy hair and crinkled clothes, when I know I haven't looked in a mirror for too long.

"You used to look at him like he was everything, way before he realised what was in front of him. I watched for years, and I knew when you started here, that he would finally notice you," she says, making me realise how smart my mum really is.

"I didn't look at him like that..." I trail off when she bursts into laughter and puts her hand on mine. I try not to blush, but knowing your mum knew about your childhood crush the whole time is a little embarrassing.

"Kennie, I just knew when your brother told us about you two getting together, that it was meant to be. Whatever happens, I know he will look after you. Much like that teacher, the twins, and even the one with the dark eyes, whose name I keep forgetting," she says.

"Enzo," I fill in the name for her and she nods, looking away from me, over the empty cafeteria to the windows. It's pouring down rain outside, the dark clouds making it look worse out there than I thought it was. You can hear the lightning shooting across the sky every now and then, and I suddenly feel a little guilty for letting East go get my phone in this weather. He only went to make sure I wouldn't go through the woods alone. I pick up my coke can, sipping from it as my mum continues talking.

"Enzo has the bad boy look going on, I half expected to see him driving a motorcycle through the academy, like Mike did when we were here," she says, making me nearly choke on my coke as I put it down next to my empty plate.

"Dad M did what?" I ask with wide eyes. I never heard about that story growing up.

"Mike was quite the bad boy back in those days, even worse than Alaric," she says, going quiet as she trails off with a sad look floating over her face. I can't imagine what she is feeling, when the hate disappears, and the realisation she doesn't have to mourn Alaric anymore. He betrayed her in the worst way, and if one my guys did that to me, I don't know if I could be as strong as she is now. I don't think I've ever looked up to my mum as much as I do right now. *She is the strongest woman I know.*

"How was he supposedly killed? You never told me and I didn't want to hurt you by asking," I ask gently, "But things are different now, and part of me wants to know when it all went wrong."

"Because he's your biological father?" she asks sadly, admitting what I don't want to hear, but I need to.

"It's clear he is, we look too much alike," I comment and she nods, holding my hand tighter, before letting go and looking down at the table.

"It was an accident; a student went out of control and I was told Alaric tried to stop him. Did I tell you that Alaric was a teacher here at the academy?" she says.

"No, I didn't know that," I say.

"He travelled back to see us every weekend because I was pregnant with you, and didn't want to give birth at the academy. I wasn't here when a very powerful teenager with eleven marks lost control near the cliffs and caused a hurricane. It killed the boy and Alaric," she sighs. "At least that's what I thought happened,".

"It's more likely he took the powerful teenager to the rebels," I say, knowing that's exactly something he would do. If he was a teacher here, then he knows all the secret artefacts, and what he needs to steal to act out his plan to use my twelfth mark.

"He wasn't always so—I don't know—crazy," she admits, looking up at me, "But he always had a dark side, a manipulative side. Don't ever trust him, he gave up his entire family, and the woman he loved for the rebels. That man will do anything for them," she warns me as the door opens and East walks in, sliding the phone with the cracked screen over to me as he sits down.

"It's got to be months since you charged that poor thing," he says, shaking his head as I turn it on. There's lots of messages and missed calls, the screen saver picture of me and Kelly, makes me want to walk out of here and demand for someone to tell me where they think she is. We are both smiling in my bedroom before we left for the academy. The start of our new lives, and yet this new life couldn't be more fucked up.

"Any news from the guys?" I ask East hopefully, who shakes his head.

"Nope, I've messaged Locke, and Enzo, but nothing. Don't worry, they will call us soon and everything will be okay," he says, placing a hand on my knee under the table. A new message pops up on my phone from an unknown number. I unlock it, freezing at the words on the screen.

*"Run, they're coming for you!"*

THAT'S ALL IT SAYS, no name or any idea who it's from. But one thing I've learnt is to never ignore someone when they tell you to run, you just run.

"We need to leave," I say, standing up quickly and turning as I hear the door open once more. I don't move as my father walks into the room, a long cloak sliding across the floor behind him, with silver marks engraved all over it. He stops, smiling widely, and looking at me like he has just won something. The smile soon disappears as my mother walks around the table, standing next to me as East gets out his chair, moving to my side.

"Alaric," is all she says in an angry tone as they stare at each other, and he shakes his head as five rebel marked walk into the room, one carrying a destroyed looking Kelly. Her hair is matted, covered in blood, and she has cuts all over her face. Her clothes are torn, and there's blood all over her. *Is she even alive?*

"You bastard," I shout, trying to step forward

222

but East stops me. Kelly lifts her head, mouthing my name before her head drops again. Her hair covering her face once more, and I have to hold in the tears that want to fall. I won't cry in front of my father, that's not happening.

"She isn't dead, you can thank me for that later, daughter," my father says, giving me a look that suggests I should say thank you.

"Thank you? I can show you where you can shove that thank you," I spit out and he shakes his head, looking back at my mum.

"Did you not teach our children any manners? Ryan is just as disappointing," he says, and the way he speaks makes me think Ryan is okay, but maybe he wouldn't work for Alaric anymore.

"I think I taught them just the right words, and to know pure bullshit when they hear it," she says, and his face goes red, "Now where the hell is my son, you piece of shit?" she asks, fury dripping from her every word as she stands strong.

"Mary Crowe, what happened to the sweet woman I loved?" he asks, clearly shocked.

"She died after her husband pretended to be dead, then he kidnapped her children, and tried to brainwash them into crazy beliefs. Now I'm not asking again, where is my son!" she shouts the end part, and he flinches a little.

"They're not crazy! You just never listened to me! We need to go back to Ariziadia, we are getting weaker all the time, and the planet will make us stronger. It will give us a chance to take back our place on earth, rather than hide on it like we aren't the most powerful ones here!" he spits out and my mum laughs.

"It's all crazy, completely crazy. The marked on Ariziadia must have the twelfth mark as they are all powerful like you say... then why haven't they opened the portal? They clearly don't want to help you, and you will lose," she says. Alaric wipes his face with his hands before pulling out a dagger from inside his cloak. He walks over to Kelly, pulls her head up by her hair, and holds the knife to her throat.

"NO!" I scream, jumping forward from East.

"Your mum and East stay here, and you come with me. Otherwise I kill her, and then them both, just like I did all your other guys," he says coldly, and I don't doubt him for a second. My mum really pissed him off, and then I pause when I process what he just said, his words making my skin freeze.

"What did you just say?" I ask, shaking my head, not believing him.

"That Daniels, those twins, and the eleven are all dead as they fell for my distraction," he laughs. "Did they really think it would be that easy? That twenty years of planning would just be over if they found us?"

"That's not true," East says, stepping next to me, and Alaric holds the knife closer to Kelly's neck, cutting her slightly, and I watch the blood drip down her front.

"It is, believe it or not. Either way we need the Academy, and Mackenzie," he tells East as I stand in complete shock, sickness filling me at the thought of the guys being in trouble. I refuse to think they are dead, I know they aren't. *I would feel it, right? Like they say people do when you lose someone you love.*

"Make your choice, we don't have much time Mackenzie," my father warns me.

"Where is Ryan?" I ask quietly, hearing Kelly whimper a little as her eyes open. She just stares at me, an empty look in her eyes. Like she has given up.

"Enough, make your choice!" he demands and I step forward, away from East and my mum, who grabs East's arm when he tries to follow me.

"I don't have a choice, just get out of here with Kelly, and mum, you heal her when you get a chance or she isn't going to make it," I tell them.

"I love you, and just hold on, we will get out and I will heal her," my mum whispers as my eyes meet East's and he doesn't have to say a word, he only nods in understanding as he looks close to breaking with fear. He doesn't stop me, and that means everything to me. He knows I couldn't live with myself if I let Kelly die and got caught anyway. I look at my father as I walk over and he lets go of Kelly, her body falling to the floor and I run to her, only to get grabbed by my arms by two of the rebels. They hold me tightly as the door opens once more and Stella walks in, a big smirk on her face as she looks around.

"They sent me to say the academy is fully under control, and the water will be ready in ten minutes," she says, "The dress is being taken out the box now."

"Very good, daughter," one of the guards holding me says and I look up at the blonde woman, seeing the similarities straight away. *They have the same bitch face, what a bad thing to inherit.*

"You bitch, your parents were never undercover, where they? You betrayed us all the whole time," I shout and she chuckles as she walks over, kicking Kelly out the way, and I glare at her as she steps right up to my face.

"I can't wait to see you in pain, the pain you deserve, and I hope my laugh is the last thing you hear, Mackenzie," she says, laughing still and then looks over at East and my mum, "I will keep East busy, don't you worry."

"I will kill you, I fucking swear to god I will," I shout at her and she slaps me hard across the face, making me stumble and taste blood in my mouth.

"Try it," she says before walking over to where East is, and my father steps in front of me so I can't see her.

"This is for your own good," he says before placing his hands on my head and pain shoots through my body, making me scream until everything goes black.

# Chapter 29

"Wake up," I hear someone whisper, something hitting my leg. I shuffle a little, feeling a tightness on my wrists like someone is grabbing me.

"Mackenzie, come on," I hear again and I blink my eyes open to the bright room, groaning at the pain spreading throughout nearly every inch of my body. I quickly remember Alaric using his pain mark on me. I look down to see handcuffs I've had on before, and I don't even need to try and use my marks. I know the handcuffs are stopping me.

"Son of a bitch," I spit out, and then hear a laugh. I turn my head to see Miss Tinder and Enzo's sister Stacy right next to me. There are two other teachers I don't know also tied up with their own handcuffs on. It was Stacy who hit my leg, and she is still laughing a little.

"If I die, at least I know my brother chose a girl with a little bit of fire," she says, winking at me.

"You won't die," I shake my head.

"How is Enzo? I only saw him for a few minutes the morning before he left to go after the rebels to rescue your friends, and we didn't have long to discuss everything. He only asked that I keep an eye on you, and make sure you didn't manage to hurt yourself while he was gone. I knew straight away that my brother had fallen for someone, and I'm happy it's someone like you," she pauses, "Someone strong enough to see past his dark and aggressive wall he puts up."

"I'm not—"

"You don't need to agree with me. I knew from my conversation with my brother how much you mean to him, even if he never said it," she says.

"He was with you that morning? I wondered why he snuck out," I say, thinking of Stella, the lying little bitch. He went to see his sister, of course he did. He wasn't with her like she said, not that I believed her anyway; Enzo isn't stupid enough to go to someone like her.

"Yes, now have you heard anything?" she demands this time, the worry for her brother showing in her eyes.

"Nothing, but I believe—I know—that he will be here to rescue us and give us a sarcastic comment about it," I say firmly and she looks away, swallowing deeply and not replying.

"Where are we?" I ask her, trying to get her attention back, and she looks over at me with watery eyes, but it's Miss Tinder that answers.

"Waiting to die, what else," she snaps.

"Why does it sound like you are blaming this on me? This isn't my fault you know, I'm tied up too," I say, and she glares at me.

"Sarcasm isn't going to help us with this situation, Miss Crowe," she snaps and then looks away. We sit silently, not hearing anything as I worry about my guys, my dads, my brother, and Kelly. And my mum, as she is with my crazy father. *How did everything go so wrong?*

"I've been wondering something, why do you and Enzo have different last names?" I ask Stacy, needing a distraction and it's the only thing that pops into my mind.

"How very random, but I'll tell you," she smiles, "Well you must know that it's a marked tradition for the men to take their woman's last name, and therefore the children the same," she says and I nod. That's why Ryan and I have the last name Crowe, and so do all my dads.

"My mother hated her last name, and didn't want to go down that route. So she had DNA tests done not long after each of us was born, and then we each had the name of our biological fathers."

"Didn't that cause a lot of trouble between you all?" I ask. There's a reason most marked decide to take the woman's last name, it stops a lot of arguments.

"I don't know. Enzo and I are close in age, and my biological father died a month after Enzo was born. My mother and two other dads, well, they lost themselves in grief and weren't the best people or parents."

"I didn't know, I'm sorry," I say.

"Don't be, but we do need to escape," she says, nodding her head towards the door of the classroom. I very much doubt we could, the room has no windows, no other doors. Its empty of anything other than us, the teachers desk and a few tables and chairs. The door opens, and two rebels walk in and come straight over to me. He grabs my arm, lifting me up off the floor, and a wave of dizziness hits me.

"Your father said to tell you to behave," he says.

"You can tell him I said fuck you," I mutter slowly, and the guards don't reply to me, but I hear Stacy's chuckle as I'm dragged from the room. We walk outside to a corridor and then straight towards the hallway, and into another room with two guards outside.

"Go in," the guard shoves me forward, and the other one opens the door, waiting for me to walk past him and into the room.

"Mackenzie, I'm glad you're awake now," Alaric says, sitting on a throne type seat in the middle of the small room. He has a book in his lap, which he closes and places on the side.

"I would have been awake sooner if you hadn't knocked me out," I spit out, and he laughs.

"We had things to do, and I couldn't trust you to be awake. Now, this is for you," he says, waving my comment off, and walking across the room to a small box. He opens it up, pulling out an awful white dress.

"A wedding dress? Fuck no, I have no intentions of marrying anyone at eighteen and certainly not in that ugly dress," I say and he snaps the box shut.

"It's not a wedding dress, it's a ceremonial dress that our ancestors wore for the ritual many years ago," he says, and walks over to me, offering me the dress.

"I'm not wearing it so you can use my twelfth power and then kill me,"

"I never wanted to kill you, there's so much you don't know, but if I have to drag your unconscious friend in here and keep hurting her until you get dressed, I will," he warns me, keeping his cold eyes on mine, and I know he means it.

"Fine," I snap, taking the dress from him.

"I will wait outside," he goes to walk away and looks back at me, "Don't do anything stupid or I will kill Kelly, and then Ryan, and then your mother. Do not test me, Mackenzie," he says and then walks out, slamming the door shut as I try not to throw something at him. I hold the dress up, smelling how it stinks of old people and dust.

"Could have at least washed it," I comment as I put it on the floor and try to pull my top off. It's a lot harder than it looks but I get it off, leaving a vest, my underwear, my boots and leggings on underneath as I pull the dress on. I get stuck half way into it, with the handcuffs catching on something, and I try to wriggle out of it, and slam into a wall.

"Ouch," I mutter, finally getting the dress on, and pulling the white lace around my ribs tighter to hold it up.

"Ready," I shout, wanting to get out this room already, and the door opens. I walk out to see Kelly being held up by two guards and I run to her, only to be caught by two rebels myself. They grip my upper arms tightly, shaking their heads at me, which I see in the corner of my eye as I keep looking at Kelly. *No one has healed her, so something must have gone wrong.*

"It's finally time," my father claps with a large grin on his face before he walks away, and we're dragged after him.

# Chapter 30

MACKENZIE

*a*s I'm dragged up to the clifftops beside the school, I can't help but think it's ironic that I thought I was safe here, when it's where they needed me all along. The water from Ariziadia underneath the school having some importance to whatever they are doing here. My long white dress drags in the mud on the ground. I stumble and the rebel dragging me catches me, holding me upright.

"Fucking watch where you're walking," he growls.

"Maybe if you weren't dragging me so quickly in the freaking dark, I wouldn't keep stumbling!" I snap. "Hell, if you didn't make me wear this ridiculous dress either, that would help," I add, practically seething. I see Kelly and the rebel dragging her catching up to us. Maybe if I can keep him talking for a moment longer...

"Fucking shut up, and come on already," he grunts, pushing me forward, and up the cliff. I almost stumble again, but keep my footing this time.

"Fine, no need to shove me," I mutter, as we continue up the last part of the trek to the clifftops.

When we reach the top, a group of rebels are already waiting there, my father included, and he's standing in the centre of the semi-circle. They're all standing around a marked-made pool of water. The edges of the pool are so flat and perfectly rounded, it has to be that someone has used their earth mark to create it and then they've filled it with water. I notice both Stella and her parents are also standing around the pool with the other marked rebels. They're all wearing stupid ceremonial robes, too. *Gods I hate those things.*

The rebel dragging me releases my arms as we reach them, going to stand next to the others. Looking behind me all I see is the edge of the cliff, and while cuffed and unable to use my marks, jumping off the edge would be extremely dumb. I feel a raindrop hit my face, and then another. As if things weren't crappy enough, it just had to be raining too.

"We all know why we are here," Alaric voice calls out, and I cringe.

*Is he really going to give a speech?* I look around hoping to see signs of the others returning here to help, to rescue me and Kelly before it's too late, but there's no sign of them. I bite my lip nervously.

"Today my daughter, Mackenzie Crowe, will open the portal to Ariziadia. We will then use the power from that world, through the opened portal, to push more power into this body of water. Water that came from Ariziadia itself," he says, pausing as if to add a dramatic flair to his speech. The winning smile on his face showing just how much he is enjoying all of this. "We will then step back into the water, as we did when we were first marked, and we will be blessed again, with enough power to rule this world the way we were meant to," he finally finishes. I expect cheering, or at least something, but they're all deadly calm and serious.

I hear Kelly whimpering as the rebel dragging her up here finally reaches the top with her. I look across at her, frowning in confusion as they walk her over to my father. As my eyes follow her, I notice one of the robed rebel's is handcuffed like I am. I frown at the figure, but their hood is up.

"Ryan?" I shout, calling across. The figure steps forward, or tries to, but he's held back by the rebels either side of him. Kelly seems to realise it's him, and she starts trying to pull towards him, but as weak as she is, she isn't able to put up much of a fight against the man pulling her towards my father. Two marked rebels move over to me. They remove the cuffs from me, but stay standing close to me so I know it would be dumb to try anything. I rub my sore wrists as I watch Alaric. He's standing way too close to Kelly for me to try and attack now that I can use my powers again, I can't risk Kelly getting hurt.

"We will now cause Mackenzie's twelfth mark to activate. We previously thought this was only achievable by physical pain, but we now know the most effective method to trigger the mark is high levels of emotion," Alaric says. *High levels of emotion, what does he—*

"No!" I scream, all thoughts cut off as his hands rest on Kelly, and her body twitches while she screams in agony.

"Let her go!" I shout, as I try to rush forward and get to her, a hand grips my shoulders tightly, holding me back and away from Kelly. I scream with her, for her, as he continues to use the pain mark on her. She collapses down in a heap on the floor in front of him. Tears are running down my face, but I don't feel my twelfth mark activating.

"Nothing, Mackenzie?" he asks, and I shake my head. *If it isn't working, maybe he'll stop?* "Do you not care for your friend at all?" he drawls, crouching down, and pulling out a knife.

"Get the fuck away from her, you monster!" I screech. I try to call on my air mark to throw the rebels holding me back off from me, but I'm so panicked I can't concentrate enough to call it properly.

Ryan manages to wriggle free from the other rebels, his hood falling down, and showing that it's him. His mouth is covered with duct tape, and his face is covered in bruises, meaning he still hasn't seen a healer. Alaric stands and turns towards Ryan.

"What do you want?" he asks, as he rips the duct tape off from Ry's mouth.

"Use me," Ryan blurts out desperately.

"No way!" I shout.

"What do you mean?" Alaric asks, looking at Ryan, paying no attention to me whatsoever as I scream.

"Use me instead of Kelly. Clearly Kenzie's powers aren't activating for Kelly being hurt. Use me instead," he pleads, his eyes looking down at Kelly sadly. "She can't take anymore. If you use the pain mark on her again or cut her with that knife, she'll die. I can take this, but not watching her die," he says. My whole body shakes with quiet sobs as I realise Ryan is trying to protect Kelly, even if it means him being tortured instead of her.

"That could work," he says, and then a loud bang comes from down below in the school. "But unfortunately, we are out of time. We're switching to plan b."

"Plan b?" Ryan echoes in a confused tone.

"There isn't enough time for torture," he answers plainly, and then he shoves the knife into Ryan's stomach. He rips it back out and then plunges it straight back in, and I scream as Ryan falls to the floor next to Kelly. I feel something in me snap, something uncontrollable taking over me. The ground beneath me shakes, and my neck burns so much that I can't help but scream. Bright, blue light shines from behind me, and I turn to face it. I gape at the plane of light shimmering into exis-tence. All the marks on my body burn hot as I stare, watching as the light becomes deeper and more corporal. It's just off the edge of the cliff, and it stretches out, getting bigger and bigger, both across and up and down. Pieces of rock fall off the cliff, floating into the air and then the cliff shakes, making us all sway as we stare. I fall to the floor, landing on my hands and knees, as I feel the power flow not just from me, but through me. It's like I'm not the creator of the power, I'm not in control, I'm just the conductor for the current. *And it's painful, so much pain.*

Turning my head, I see the rebels rushing forward, and Kelly is dragged with them. I feel drowsy, but shouldn't I be dead? I thought using the twelfth mark kills you, and the portal is right there, I should be dead... *Dead...Ryan! I have to help him!*

I pull myself into a standing position, and push through the marked that are staring at the portal with wide eyes. Once I reach my brother, I fall to my knees next to him, throwing my hands over the wound in his stomach trying to stop the blood. It slips through my fingers and runs down onto my dress. The rain pours down even heavier than before, and I can feel my wet hair sticking to the sides of my face and the back of my neck, but I don't care.

"Please be okay, please," I whisper, tears streaming down my face.

"Forgive me," he whispers, and I realise I've seen this all before. Kelly's vision. *Gods, please no.*

"There's nothing to forgive, just don't die, okay? I love you, so you can't die," I reply. My hands glow as I call on my healing, putting all my strength into it. My healing mark burns on my skin, so fucking hot I scream. I can hear shouts, familiar voices, but I fall back as all the marks on my body begin to burn. I stare down at the marks on my wrists, gaping in disbelief as they begin to fade, leaving my skin bare. *I'm no longer marked.*

The cliff shakes once more, a massive quake, and I stare down at Ryan as his head falls to the side.

"NO!" I scream, shaking him and begging for my healing mark to come back, for anyone to help. *But no one comes.* Everything in me just breaks as I fall backwards collapsing, my eyes closing but the image of my brother dying never leaves my mind.

---

"SHE'S COMING AROUND," I hear Kelly sob, "I won't lose her too, I'd die first," she says. I sit up with a gasp, feeling every part of me hurting a little but it's not too bad. Kelly is sitting next to me, tears pouring down her face as she sobs into her hands. I look in front of me to see my mum holding Ryan close to her and I can't seem to look away as she turns to me but is silent.

"Who?" I ask, standing up shaky with Kelly's help and the sight in front of me is madness.

"He died to save me, didn't he?" Kelly whispers, and I give her a shaky nod, not trusting my words.

"Go, I have your brother and will keep him safe. Help them destroy Alaric," my mum finally says, holding him close, and I know it's pointless to point out she can't keep him safe now. He is dead but one look at my mum, just makes me realise that she is right. Ryan can't die for nothing.

"Oh god Ry," she says, covering her face with her hands as she cries. I hold her to me, trying not to cry myself as I look around. Rebels and marked are fighting each other, the portal is open, showing a land full of massive trees and what looks like a rain forest. The cliff is falling apart, slowly bits of it are flying into the portal from the pressure. I slam us both to the floor as a giant wave of fire shoots through the sky above our heads. Kelly rolls next to me, looking around like I am.

"It's madness, I can't see a thing," I tell her.

"Them," Kelly points to my left, where right on the edge of the cliff is Mr Daniels, East, and the twins fighting my father and ten other rebels. They are being pushed back with every attack against them, and not landing any hits on my father at all by the looks of it. I run towards them, only to get hit by a wave of air that sends me flying. I bounce across the floor, trying to call my marks as I roll to stop and remember I don't have them anymore.

"Kenzie!" I hear shouted through the fighting, and I pull myself up, and then duck as a large rock floats above my head and towards the portal. I turn around in a circle, not seeing anyone I know and then I spot my guys again, this time Kelly is with them, leaning on the floor and healing someone I can't see. Someone has put a ward up around them all, and the rebels are throwing fire and water at it constantly, making it impossible to really see them. I watch as my father leans down on the ground, placing his hands in the ground and the ground cracks. I run towards them, but I'm too late as my father uses his earth mark to throw the ground, that Kelly and the guys are on, straight into the portal. I hear them shout, Kelly scream, and then there's an eerie silence.

"No!" I shout, running straight at my father and he turns, smiling at me. He lifts his hand, using his air mark to control my body, and pull it towards him. I fight, struggling against him but it's no use. I'm basically human now.

"My daughter, how very useful you are, but we have a problem. I can't trust you, I wish I could," he says, pulling me closer to him, and then turning us around.

"Have fun in Ariziadia, I'm sure the marked people there will be welcoming to you," he says and then lets me go over the cliff. I scream, stretching my hands out and catching anything I can, and finally grabbing something.

My fingers scrape across the ledge, holding on as the portal behind me pulls me to it. I glance down, only regretting doing so as I see the swirling blue portal and my grip on the edge of the stone slips. I hold in a scream as I try to get a better grip, only the blood on my hands is making it impossible to hold on. The stupid white dress I'm wearing only makes it harder for me to use my feet to climb up.

"Kenzie!" I hear Enzo shouting my name. I try to look up, only to have to use my hand to push a piece of rock that flies at my head away from me. I know Enzo won't stop looking for me, even in all the madness of the flying pieces of rocks that are being pulled into the portal, and the chance he could die before he finds me.

"Enzo, here!" I shout back, and I see him look over the edge of the cliff I fell down. Enzo jumps, landing right in front of me on the ledge and reaches down, pulling me up into his arms.

"I've got you, it's okay," he says and gently kisses my forehead.

"No, it's too late, Ryan is dead, the portal is open, and everyone fell in the portal to god knows where," I mumble, shaking my head and Enzo squeezes me tighter.

"You couldn't have changed anything about what happened," I hear Enzo say, but I'm too distracted to tell him he is wrong as someone jumps down, and lands next to us. Enzo turns us so he is slightly in front of me as we face my father. He stands there, with his long coat blowing in the wind and a happy expression. He won.

"It's your fault," I spit out and he laughs.

"Good bye, Mackenzie. Thank you for everything you have done for this world, but I'm afraid we don't need you anymore," he says in a cruel, emotionless voice. I'm too late to try and stop him when he shoots a blast of air at me and Enzo, sending us flying off the edge of the ledge, and down into the portal. The last thing I see is Enzo pulling me to his chest and his dark eyes as he looks down at me.

**THE END**

*The Story continues in book 3, Marked by Destruction.*

## About the Authors:

**Cece Rose** is the proud owner of one dog, four turtles and one annoying boyfriend.

She hails from Devon in the South-West of England but dreams of sunny skies and sand between her toes. Although, whenever abroad she will moan about the heat and the sand that gets everywhere.

She has largely convinced all who know her that she is a vampire, mainly due to her nocturnal habits. In reality, it's because her creativity only ever strikes when the sky is dark, and the stars are shining. (Plus, it's actually quiet enough to concentrate on writing.)

You can find Cece on Facebook and Twitter. **And don't forget to join her Demon Den!**

**G. Bailey** lives in rainy (sometimes sunny) England with her husband, two children, one slightly strange cat.

When she isn't writing (which is unusual), she can be found reading one of the many books in her house or talking to her amazing readers.

She has a slight addiction to Ben & Jerry's ice cream and chocolate.

Please feel free to stalk her, in her group, <u>Bailey's Pack</u>.

<u>Facebook</u>---<u>Twitter</u>---<u>Website</u>

*PS. A big thank you to Kayla Erickson, for helping us find a name for a certain character.*

Other Titles by Cece Rose

**The Desdemona Chronicles-**

A Demon's Blade (Book One)

A Demon's Debt (Book Two)

An Angel's Defiance (Coming Soon)

**Fated Serial**

Fractured Fate (Part One)

Twisted Fate (Part Two)

Rejecting Fate (Part Three)

Accepting Fate (Coming soon)

**The Last Siren's Song**

Blood Sea (Book One)

Blood Moon (Coming Soon)

**Souls of Creatures Series**

Vengeance (Book One)

Justice (Coming Soon)

**Snow and Seduction Anthology**

Snowflake (standalone)

**The Marked Series - with G. Bailey**

Marked by Power (Book One)

Marked by Pain (Book Two)

Marked by Destruction (Book Three)

Other Titles by G. Bailey

**The King Brothers Series-**

Izzy's Beginning (Book one)

Sebastian's Chance (Book two)

Elliot's Secret (Book three)

Harley's Fall (Book Four)

Luke's Revenge (Coming soon)

**Her Guardians Series-**

Winter's Guardian (Book one)

Winter's Kiss (Book two)

Winter's Promise (Book three)

Winter's War (Book Four)

**Her Fate Series-**

*(Her Guardians Series spinoff)*

Adelaide's Fate (Coming soon)

**Saved by Pirates Series-**

Escape the sea (Book One)

Love the sea (Book Two)

Save the sea (Coming soon)


**One Night series-**

Strip for me (Book one)

Live for Me (Coming soon)


**The Marked Series (Co-written with Cece Rose)-**

Marked by Power (Book one)

Marked by Pain (Book two)

Marked by Destruction (Book Three)


**Snow and Seduction anthology-**

Triple Kisses


**The Forest Pack series-**

Run Little Wolf- (Book One)

**Protected by Dragons series-**

Wings of Ice- (Book One)

Wings of Fire (Coming Soon)

Please continue reading for two short samples of
individual works from the authors!
You can pre-order Blood Sea on amazon now by
clicking here.
You can pre-order Wings of Ice on amazon now by
clicking here.

# Blood Sea

*Don't go in the water; Never go out at night.*
*For in the seas and darkness, are creatures that will bite.*
I've always been drawn to the water, sneaking away
to swim in the hidden cove. I know the dangers, but
the water calls to me, its song luring me into the
depths.
All my life I've been home by dark, but just once I
want to swim in the moonlight. The vampires
haven't come to our isle in years anyway, it's a
stupid precaution to stay inside.
How could I know that the one night I choose to
take a moonlit swim, the waters around our island
would run red with blood?

## Blood Sea Prologue

His black pupils dilate wide, covering the blue irises of his eyes and stretching out to fill the whites, so all I can see is black. I try to dart away, but he grips my shoulders tightly, holding me firmly in place. "Do not fucking talk to me like that, Azula. You have no power here. This is my ship, and you will do as I say."

"I'll talk however I damn well please, you aren't my captain," I retort brazenly. I regret the words after they've left my mouth, though, as his grip tightens on my shoulders. The thought occurs to me that I should probably be a lot more afraid than I am, and I should definitely start acting a little smarter if I want to make it out of here alive.

"While you're aboard my ship, I'm the authority because I'm the captain. I am the fucking god of all that lies aboard this vessel. Do you understand me, Azula?" he asks. His voice is low, not needing to shout to make his point. The power in his words is enough on its own. Shaking slightly in his grip, I manage to nod, licking my suddenly dry lips to moisten them. "Tell me that you understand," he demands, my nod clearly not enough for him.

My mouth feels so dry as I try to summon words. I can barely breathe, my heart racing with fear. I can't look away from his pitch-black eyes, and I couldn't even move if I did try with his hands keeping me in place.

"I understand," I whisper.

"I understand, Captain," he corrects me, and he leans down closer, his face inches from mine as he does.

"I understand... Captain," I choke out. He draws away, releasing me and stepping back a few paces.

"You will stay in here and not cause any trouble until we reach land. Once there you will leave, and I or my crew will never see you again, do you understand?" he questions.

"I understand perfectly." He steps closer again and my heart jumps in my chest from fright. "I understand perfectly, Captain," I correct myself, taking a deep breath in and out.

"Good. There's a bed behind the curtain there, rest for now. Whatever you do, do not cut yourself on anything. You cannot let your blood spill. If it does, I will not be able to keep the crew away from you," he says as he heads for the door.

"Yes, Captain," I reply quietly, and he nods, hearing my words. "How far away from land are we? And what port do we near?" I ask, my voice coming back to me easier now that he's on the other side of the cabin and about to leave.

"A few days at most, depending on the winds. We are passing by Asmia, and it is there we will leave you before continuing on our way," he answers. "Now sleep," he commands, leaving and closing the door with a slam behind him.

## Blood Sea Chapter One

Smiling across the dinner table at James, I ignore our two fathers' droning on about the merchant ships troubles at seas, not that I ever really pay much attention. James is dressed more formally than usual—the mix of white, black, and bright, royal blue standing out against his sun-kissed skin and pale eyes. His usually messy, dark blond hair has been tamed, the natural highlights showing off even more than usual. I feel his foot nudge mine under the table, I nudge his back and bite my lip to keep in laughter from the amused look on his face.

"Azula, are you listening to what Mr Burcham has said?" my father asks me, snapping my attention away from James.

"Sorry? What was that, Mr Burcham, I didn't

quite catch it?" I ask, smiling innocently. My father sighs, not falling for it for an instant. I tune back out as James' father starts talking again. I take a sip of the ridiculous wine they brought over to be polite. It tastes like bath salts and I try not to gag as I swallow it.

"Azula," my father says again.

"Yes, daddy?" I ask, turning back to face him again.

"Do you have anything to say about what Mr Burcham has kindly repeated for you?" he asks. I shrug.

"Not really," I reply, taking another sip of the fowl wine to escape more small talk. As much as I enjoy James' company, his father is a total bore and speaks about the same topics every time they come for dinner. Thankfully, I learnt to tune out the drivel years ago; James had too.

"Do you not find it the least bit concerning that...*blah blah blah,*" I tune him back out. What is there to possibly find concerning about the state of affairs more than usual. The seas run red with blood, and we hide in our homes at night. We're terrified victims just waiting to slip up. I'm sick of it, I want to live and do as I please. Better to enjoy a short life than to loathe every minute of a long one. There is nothing interesting about our small island, I want to explore and see the world, but my father barely lets me out of the house. My chances of ever escaping Carysi are minimal at best. Our closest neighbouring island, Smoke, is uninhabited, due to the volcanic activity that has wrecked any previous attempt at life there. The second closest is Eska. Eska is the home to trade, and bustling streets, or so James tells me. One day, I will get to see it, I won't let him stop me. Just because of the near constant raids on the sea boarding towns and ports, they think it's no place for a woman to go. When I argue that women do live in those towns, the response is always they're a *different* kind of woman. I barely resist huffing aloud at the thought.

"I'm feeling quite full; would you mind letting me be excused?" I ask, already standing. My father sighs again, scratching at the grey stubble on his face.

"Fine, sweetheart, but stay inside the manor; it'll be dark soon."

"Of course, I was just thinking of going to read in the library," I reply, knowing full well he will never go in there and check. He never steps into that room, he says it reminds him too much of my mother. I walk across and place a kiss on his cheek, before striding out the room, certain that James will quickly follow.

I wait at the end of the corridor, and sure enough, a few minutes later James exits the room and meets me at the edge. I slide my hands into his and draw him close. Leaning up and placing a kiss to lips quickly, before pulling away and stepping back.

"Come on, I've got something fun planned," I greet him.

"Fun? I should be terrified, right?" he replies teasingly.

"When is being scared ever not fun?" I reply, leading the way through the large building I call home. I lead him to the secret exit, tucked away behind a large painting of the sea is the tunnel that leads right out to the small cove. It had once been used for smuggling, before the human pirates were all but wiped out anyway.

"It's a bit late to be sneaking out, Zu," he says, following me down the pathway anyway.

"I just want to go for a quick dip in the water, Jay," I reply, trailing my fingers along the wall in the darker parts of the tunnel to make sure I don't walk into anything. Not that I really need to, I know the route from memory by now, considering I sneak down here most days to take a dip in the sea. I try not to feel guilty about my secret, but I know that not even James would approve of me sneaking down here by myself. He thinks we only ever come down together, but I doubt I could stay away from the water for that long to wait for the days when he's here.

"We won't have long if we're going to be inside by dark, Zu," he says.

"What if we aren't inside by dark?" I ask.

"Don't be ridiculous, that's way too dangerous," he answers.

"Why is it? They haven't bothered this island for years. It's been years since they raided here and yet we all still hide away in our homes. How is this any different to us going in the sea during the day? We're not supposed to do that either," I reply, challengingly, not slowing my pace as we walk through the dark.

"You know it's different. We never go out too deep, if something happened we could always get to shore and with the sun up, there's nothing they could do once we reached the land," he says.

"It will be fine, don't be such a bore, James. I

thought you were more interesting than your two brothers," I reply, trying to hit the right nerves to get my way. James was easily far more interesting than his two older brothers. William and Archie were two of the most boring people I'd ever had the displeasure of meeting, they ranked up there with Mr Burcham himself. It was a wonder James had come out as interesting as he had. I like to credit that to all the time he spent with me growing up, but he'd always been like a spark in my life.

"You know that I am far more interesting than those two fools," he mutters. I stop and turn to face him as we reach the opening to the cove.

"Then prove it, what have we got to lose? Just this one time, let's take a dip in the moonlight?" I offer, stepping close. "It could be romantic," I add slyly.

"Fine, what's the worst that could happen?" he says, giving into my demands as always. I smile and slide into his arms.

"This is going to be so much fun," I whisper in his ear, as I tug off his blue jacket, letting it fall onto the sandy ground.

"That's what you always say before getting me into trouble," he replies wryly.

"And yet you keep following me," I tease.

"I'll follow you anywhere, Zu," he replies sincerely. And I know he would, James has been in love with me for years after all.

## Wings of Ice

*Four Dragon Guards. Three Curses. Two Heirs. One Choice...*
*Forbidden love or the throne of the dragons?*

Isola Dragice thought she knew what her future would bring. On her eighteenth birthday, she'd inherit the dragon throne, but one earth-shattering moment destroys everything.

As war looms heavy over Dragca, Isola is catapulted

out of her pretend human life and thrust into a world, she knows little of. One life-threatening accident, when she loses control of her dragon, ends up with the whole of Dragca Academy hating her.

When the four most powerful dragons in history are ordered to protect her, they find themselves with an awkward problem. Her family cursed them centuries ago, relegating them to slaves of the throne and they hate all royals. Especially an ice dragon princess with no control over her powers that can kill fire dragons. Which the whole school is full of.

*What happens when fire falls for Ice?*

## Wings of Ice Prologue

Everything inside me screams as I run through the doors of the castle, seeing the dead dragons lining the floors and the sight making me sick to my stomach. I try not to look at the spears in their stomachs, the dragonglass that is rare in this world. *Where did they get it?* The more and more bodies I pass, who are both dragon and guards, the less hope I have that my father is okay. *No, I can't be too late, I can't lose*

*him too.* The once grand doors to the throne room are smashed into pieces of stone, in a pile on the floor, and only the hinges to the door hang off the walls. I run straight over, climbing over the rocks and broken stone. The sight in front of me makes me stop, not believing what I'm seeing but I know it's true.

"Father..." I ask quietly, knowing he won't reply to me. My father is sat on his throne, a sword through his stomach and a wide mouthed expression on his face. His blood drips down onto the gold floors of the throne room and snow falls from the broken ceiling above onto his face. There's no ice in here, no sign he even tried to fight before he was killed. He must have never saw this coming because he trusted whoever killed him.

"No," is I can think to say as I fall to my knees, bending my head and looking down at the ground instead of the body of my father. I couldn't stop this, even when they warned me and risked everything. I hear footsteps in front of me as I watch my tears drip onto the ground, but I don't look up as I know who it is. I know from the way they smell, my dragon whispers to me their name but I can't even think it.

"Why?" I ask as everything clicks into place. I

should have known, I should have never had trusted him.

"Because the curse has to end. Because he was no good for Dragca. Our city needs a true heir, me. I'm the heir of fire and ice, the one the prophecy speaks of and it's finally time I took what is mine," he says and every word seems to cut straight through my heart. *I trusted him.*

"The curse hasn't ended, I'm still here," I whisper to the dragon in front of me but I know he could hear my words like I just spoke them into his ear.

"Not for long, not even for moment longer actually. Your dragon guard will only thank me when you are gone. I didn't want to do this to you, not in the end, but you are too powerful. You are no use to me anymore, not unless you're gone," he says. I look down at the ground as his words run around my head and I don't know what to do. I feel lost, powerless and broken in every way possible. There's a part of the door in front of me that catches my attention, a part with the royal crest on. The dragon in a circle, a proud, strong dragon. My father's words come back to me and I know they are all I need to say.

"There's a reason ice dragons hold the throne

and have done for centuries. There's a reason the royal name Dragice is feared." I say and stand up slowly, wiping my tears away.

"We don't give up and we bow to no one. I'm Isola Dragice, and you will pay for what you have done," I tell him as finally meet his now cruel eyes, before calling my dragon and feeling her take over.

## Wings of Ice Chapter One

"Isola!" I hear shouted from the stairs but I keep my headphones on as I stare at my laptop and pretend I didn't hear her shout my name for the tenth time. The music blasts around my head as I try to focus on history paperback that is due in tomorrow.

"Isola, will you take those things out and listen to me?" Jules shouts at me again, and I pop one of my headphones out as I look up at her. She stands at the end of my bed, her hands on her hips and her glasses branched on the end of her nose. Her long grey hair is up in a tight bun, and she has an old styled dress that looks like flowers threw up on. Jules is my house sitter, or babysitter as I like to call her. I don't think I need a baby sitter at seventeen, not when I'm eighteen in two days anyway, and can look after myself.

"Both headphones out, I want them both out when you listen to me," she says and I knew this was coming. I pull the headphones out and pause the music on my phone.

"I did try to clean up after the party, I swear," I say and she raises her eyebrows.

"How many teenagers did you have in here? Ten? A hundred?" she says and I shrug my shoulders as I sit up on the bed and cross my legs.

"I don't know, it's all a little fuzzy," I reply honestly. My head is still pounding and I know it was the wine, or the tequila shots. Who knows? I look up again as she shakes her head at me, speaking a sentence in Spanish that I can't understand but I doubt it's nice. I don't think I want to hear what she has to says about the party I threw last night anyway. I look around my simple room, seeing the dressing table, the wardrobe, the bed I'm sitting on. There isn't much in here that is personal, no photos or anything that means anything to me.

"Miss Jules, looking as beautiful as always," Jace says, in an overly sweet tone as he walks into my bedroom. He walks straight over to Jules and kisses her cheek, making her giggle. Jace is that typical hot guy, with his white blonde hair and crystal blue eyes. Even my sixty year old house sitter can't be mad at him for long, he can charm just about anyone.

"Don't start with that pouty cute face," she tuts at him and he widens his arms, pretending to be shocked.

"What face? I'm always like this," he says and she laughs, any anger she had disappearing.

"I'm going to clean up this state of a house and you should leave, you're going to be late for school. I don't want to have to tell your father that when I tell him about the party," she says as she points a finger at me and I hold in the urge to laugh. She emails my father all the time about anything I do but he never responds. He just pays her to keep the house running and to make sure I don't get into too much trouble. I doubt if he doesn't have the time to talk to me in the last ten years, he isn't going to have the time to email a human he hired. Jules walks out the room and Jace leans against the wall, tucking his hands into his pockets. I run my eyes over his tight jeans, his white shirt that is ridden up a little to show his toned stomach and finally to his handsome face that is grinning at me. He knows exactly what he does to me.

"You look too sexy when you do that," I comment and he grins.

"Isn't that the point? Now come and give your boyfriend a kiss," he teases and I do a fake sigh before getting up and walking over to him. I lean up, brushing my lips against his cold ones and he smiles, kissing me back just as gently.

"We should go but I was wondering if you wanted to go to the mountains this weekend and try some flying?" he asks and I blank my expression before walking away from him and towards the mirror hanging on the wall near the door. I smooth my wavy, shoulder length blonde hair down and it just bounces back up, ignoring me. My blue eyes stare back at me, bright and crystal clear. Jace says it's like looking into a mirror when he looks into my eyes, they are so clear. I check out my jeans and tank top, and grabbing my leather coat from where it hangs on the back of the door before answering Jace.

"I've got a lot of homework to do-" I say and he shakes his head as he cuts me off.

"-Issy, when was the last time you let her out? It's been, what months?" he asks and I turn away, walking out my bedroom door and hearing him sigh behind me.

"Issy, we can't avoid this forever. Not when we have to go back in two weeks," he reminds me and I stop, leaning my head back against the plain white walls of the corridor.

"I know we have to go back. We have to train to rule a race we know nothing about just because of who our parents are. Don't you ever want to run away, hide in the human world we have been left in for all these years?" I ask, feeling a grumble of anger from my dragon inside my mind. I quickly slam down the barrier between me and my dragon in my head, stopping her from contacting me, no matter how much it hurts me to do so. I can't let her control me.

"Issy, we were left here so we would be safe. We are the last ice dragons and our parents had no choice. Plus... being a dragon around humans is a nightmare, you know that," he says, stepping closer to me.

"I don't want to rule, I don't want anything to do with Dragca," I say, looking away.

"I guess its lucky we have each other, ruling on our own would have been a disaster," he says, stepping in front of me so I can't move and he gently kisses my forehead.

"I know. I just don't want to go back, to see my father and everything that has to come with that," I say, and he steps back to tilt my head up to look at him.

"You're the heir to the throne of the dragons. You're the princess of Dragca. Your life was never meant to be here with the humans," he says and I move away from him, not replying because I know he sees it differently to how I do. He is the ice prince, and his parents call him every week. I haven't spoken to any of my family in ten years and I have never stepped back into Dragca since then. It's the only thing we disagree on, our future.

"Issy, let's just have a good day and then maybe I could get you that peanut bacon sandwich you love from the deli?" he suggests, running to catch up with me on the stairs.

"Now you're talking," I grin at him as he hooks

an arm around my waist and leans down to whisper in my ear,

"And I could do that thing with my tongue that you…" he gets cut off when Jules opens the door in front of us, clearing her throat and ushers us out as we laugh.